WITCHY TALES

A WICKED WITCHES OF THE MIDWEST FANTASY
BOOK ONE

AMANDA M. LEE

WINCHESTERSHAW PUBLICATIONS

Copyright © 2015 by Amanda M. Lee

All rights reserved.

No part of this book may be reproduced in any form or by any electronic or mechanical means, including information storage and retrieval systems, without written permission from the author, except for the use of brief quotations in a book review.

❦ Created with Vellum

Once upon a time there were three little girls, and they annoyed their great-aunt very much.

– *Aunt Tillie's Wonderful World of Stories to Make Little Girls Shut Up*

CHAPTER 1

"What's going on?"

I glanced up from the porch swing, my eyes landing on handsome perfection, and smiled by way of greeting as my boyfriend Landon Michaels climbed the steps of my family's inn. He stooped low to give me a kiss and then lifted my feet and settled beside me.

"You're early this weekend," I said.

An agent working out of the FBI's Traverse City field office in northern Lower Michigan, he generally split his time between his apartment there and the guesthouse I shared with my cousins here in Hemlock Cove. Although, truth be told, he was increasingly finding reasons to spend more nights with me as the weeks progressed. I'm not complaining, mind you. I've just noticed he's around a lot more, which seems to make both of us happy.

"I got up at the crack of dawn so I could finish all of my paperwork and be here in time for dinner," Landon said, pushing his longish black hair from his face and fixing his warm eyes on me. "I might have missed you a little."

"You just saw me yesterday morning," I reminded him.

"Yes, but you were still asleep when I left," Landon said. "You made a weird growling sound and rolled over when I kissed you. I felt bereft without a proper goodbye."

He likes to mess with me. "I still saw you."

"But then I had to go all day yesterday without seeing you, and I had to spend the night in my sad little apartment all alone, and then I had to go through today without my daily Bay fix. It was something out of a nightmare."

He was teasing me, but he was so cute it didn't really matter. He does something weird to my heart. I can't explain it. I just feel ... lighter ... when he's around.

My name is Bay Winchester, and I'm a witch in love. Sure, the witch stuff is a pain to deal with, but the love stuff is getting easier to get a handle every day.

"I know you think you're being a drama queen and that it's somehow funny, but I'm choosing to take your words at face value," I said, leaning forward and lightly pressing my lips against his strong chin. "I'll now be able to spend the next few days picturing you curled up in a little ball crying because you had to sleep alone."

Landon grinned, the expression lighting his already handsome face. "I only cried a little."

"Did your mascara run?"

"You're not funny." Landon reached over and tickled my ribs, delighting when he heard me laugh until I gasped for relief.

"Stop that," I ordered. "It's starting to hurt."

Landon narrowed his eyes as he tried to determine whether I was playing him or telling the truth. Finally, he opted to pull his hand away. "I think you're making that up, but I would never hurt you, so I'm going to stop."

"That's good," I said.

"Why?"

"Then I can do this." I launched myself on him, using my weight to push him back on the swing and force him down so I could return the tickling favor. Exertion clouded Landon's angular face as he grappled to shift my body so he was back in control. I'm stronger than I look, though.

"Oh, good grief, do I have to get the hose?"

I glanced up, Landon's hand tight on my hip as the wickedest witch in the Midwest sauntered onto the front porch of The Overlook – and yes, when my mother announced she and her sisters were naming the inn that, I tried to explain why it was a bad idea. They either didn't get it, or didn't care.

"Aunt Tillie," Landon said, grimacing when I poked my finger into his ribs again. "How are you this fine summer evening?"

"Well, my arthritis is acting up, my glaucoma is taking over and my hemorrhoids have a mind of their own," Aunt Tillie said. "Other than that, I'm just peachy."

"You don't have glaucoma," I said. "You need to stop telling people that. That's your excuse for planting a pot field, even though we all know you're a senior citizen who likes to burn a big blunt from time to time."

Landon arched an eyebrow. "Burn a big blunt? Where did you learn the lingo?"

"She's been watching *The Wire* with me," Aunt Tillie said. "On the nights you're not here and Clove and Thistle are busy with Marcus and Sam, she has nothing better to do than hang out with me. It's pitiful."

I frowned while Landon fought to hide his smile. "I don't think I'm the only one crying when we're apart," he teased. "You must be desperate to spend your nights with Netflix and Aunt Tillie."

"I'll have you know I'm a very popular person," I said. "I could hang out with a lot of people."

"Are any of them alive?"

Talking to ghosts was one of my witchy gifts. Landon wasn't always happy with my abilities, but he was putting up a good effort to understand them these days. "I'm desirable," I said. "I could have any number of male suitors the second I snap my fingers."

Landon wrinkled his nose. "Why don't we just agree that I'm the only one masochistic enough to put up with this family? And why don't we go inside and get a drink?"

I poked him again, this time a little more viciously. "Tell me I'm desirable."

"I desire you all the time," Landon said, laughing. "I still think I'm a saint for putting up with this ... nonsense."

"You shouldn't put up with that lip," Aunt Tillie said. "If he was in my bed I'd glue his lips together just to get him to shut up."

Landon shuddered, the mental image of sharing a bed with Aunt Tillie clearly throwing him for a loop. "Don't ever say anything like that again."

"Oh, please, you know very well you've had dreams about sharing a bed with me," Aunt Tillie chided. "Don't deny it. The Goddess knows when you're lying ... and she doesn't like it."

"I don't know why I come back here weekend after weekend when all I get is abuse," Landon said, pushing me up so we could both settle into a more comfortable sitting position. "It must be because I'm such a masochist."

I pinched him one more time for good measure and then focused my attention on Aunt Tillie. "What's up with you? Why are you out here? Isn't *Jeopardy* set to start in five minutes?"

One thing you don't want to do is get between Aunt Tillie and Alex Trebek. She takes it personally. She thinks she knows all of the answers, and then swears the television is lying when she's wrong. Winchesters like to be right. All of us.

"I needed some fresh air," Aunt Tillie said.

"Why?"

"Because ... well ... why does it matter? I love nature. Give it a rest."

She was up to something. I can always tell. The first hint is the fact that she's breathing. The second is her darting eyes when formulating a lie on the spot.

"Why don't I believe you?" Landon asked.

"Because you're suspicious by nature," Aunt Tillie replied, nonplussed. "It's your biggest personality flaw."

"How many personality flaws do I have?" Landon asked.

"None," I said, patting his hand reassuringly. "She's making that up."

"Six," Aunt Tillie countered.

Landon lifted an eyebrow. "Six?"

"You have a big ego, you're a bully when you want to be, you yell too much, you're a glutton, and I think you might be a sexual deviant," Aunt Tillie said.

"That's on top of me being suspicious, right?"

"Exactly."

"Well, I can't argue with any of that," Landon said. "You know you have some of the same personality defects, right?"

"I don't have any personality defects," Aunt Tillie said, crossing her arms over her chest.

I tried to swallow the snort before it escaped and failed.

"I don't," Aunt Tillie said. "I'm one of those rare people who have no failings."

"Good to know," Landon said.

Something else was going on here. "Why are you really out here?"

"I told you, I want to enjoy nature," Aunt Tillie said. "Summers are far too short in Michigan. I want to enjoy this one before winter returns."

"I ... ."

"Aunt Tillie!"

The three of us froze when we heard the bellow. By the time Landon and I shifted our eyes back to Aunt Tillie, she was already descending the porch steps.

"You never saw me," she said.

The front door of The Overlook flew open and my mother stormed out, her sisters, Marnie and Twila, close on her heels. "You stop right there," Mom ordered.

Aunt Tillie did as she was told, but instead of turning to face her family she focused on a nearby tree and pasted a puzzled look on her face. "I think we should hire someone to come in and prune some of these trees," she said. "The ones over here are getting out of control."

"You're out here looking at the trees?" Mom asked, dubious. "Do you really expect us to believe that?"

"What's going on?" Thistle asked, walking up to the front porch from the path on the west side of The Overlook. Her boyfriend Marcus was beside her, and our other cousin, Clove, trailed several feet behind with her boyfriend Sam.

"I have no idea," I said. "We were hanging out when she came outside and said she was hankering for some nature."

"And you believed her?" Marnie asked.

"Of course not."

"You're on my list," Aunt Tillie said, shooting me a dark look and extending a gnarled finger in my direction. "You're at the top of it."

Thistle clapped her hands excitedly. "I'm so glad. I've been at the top of the list for weeks."

"You've been at the top of the list since you were born," Aunt Tillie said. "It's in your nature to be at the top of the list. You want to excel in everything."

"Let's get back on topic," Mom suggested.

"Let's," Aunt Tillie agreed. "I think these trees need to be pruned."

"That's not the topic I was talking about," Mom said.

Aunt Tillie ignored her. "Marcus, I don't suppose you would be willing to help me prune these trees, would you?"

"Sure," Marcus said, his face impassive. "I like pruning trees."

"You're multifaceted weird," Thistle said.

Marcus leaned over and gave her a quick kiss. "That's why we get along so well."

"Well, that was annoying enough to put you right back at the top of my list," Aunt Tillie said, rolling her eyes. "Don't worry, Marcus, I wasn't talking about you."

The only adult Aunt Tillie never seems to lose her temper with is Marcus. She's also particularly fond of Annie, the daughter of a woman who works at the inn, but Marcus has a special place in her heart. They have an interesting relationship.

"Does anyone want to tell me what's going on here?" Landon asked. "I have a feeling you guys came out here for a reason."

"We have a very big reason," Mom said. "Do you know who was on the phone, Aunt Tillie? I think you do. That's why you scampered out of the house like you did."

"I'm sure I have no idea what you're talking about," Aunt Tillie said.

"Who was on the phone?" I asked. Knowing Aunt Tillie, she could be up to almost anything.

"It was a sales representative from Manchester Printing in Traverse City," Mom said. "He told me that her order of a thousand labels – the ones for her new wine business, mind you – were on their way and they would be here tomorrow."

Uh-oh. Aunt Tillie's wine business was a sore spot. Everyone, including Landon, knew she made it illegally. He'd been trying to shut her down for months, but he kept running into brick walls. Most of those walls were short and Aunt Tillie-shaped.

"Why would you need a thousand wine labels?" Thistle asked, confused. "You generally only make twenty bottles at a time."

"How do you know that?" Landon asked, his eyes narrowing. "Have you been helping her?"

"Don't get all huffy with me," Thistle said. "She's been making wine for decades. She used to make us help when we were teenagers."

"Yeah, we were in charge of the sugar and yeast," Clove said.

"And the manual labor of filling the bottles and waxing the corks," I added.

Landon scowled. "I can't listen to this," he said. "She's illegally making wine and now you're telling me she used underage kids to do her dirty work? What do you expect me to do with that?"

"Ignore it," Mom said.

"What's in the past is in the past," Marnie said. "You know very well you can't arrest her for things she did more than a decade ago."

One look at Landon's face told me he might have known it in his head but his heart was putting up a fight.

"Why do you need a thousand bottles of wine?" I asked.

"I'm … expanding my business," Aunt Tillie said. "I'm taking them to a consignment fair tomorrow afternoon."

"You are not," Landon said. "That's illegal. You cannot sell that wine. It's one thing to illegally make it and drink it yourself. It's another to sell it. I can't sit by and watch you sell it."

I put my hand on his arm to still him. "What consignment fair sells wine?"

"It's a special one over in Kingston," Aunt Tillie said, studying her fingernails.

"She's talking about the Renaissance fair," Thistle said. "I saw it advertised on a billboard. I was going to suggest that we all go, but then I got distracted by ... this."

I glanced at Landon. "Can she sell homemade wine at a Renaissance fair?"

"Not that I'm aware of," he said. "She needs a permit."

"I have a permit."

"Where did you get a permit?"

Aunt Tillie shrugged. "The permit fairies?"

Thistle chortled. "I'm guessing she used that computer Bay gave her to conjure one up."

Whoops. That computer gift kept coming back to bite me on the ... .

"You're not selling that wine," Landon said. "I can promise you that. I'll be up here before dawn, and you're not taking that wine anywhere. I can't willingly let you leave when I know you're going to be committing a crime."

"I don't need your permission to run my own business," Aunt Tillie said. "I'm an adult. I can do what I want."

"You're not doing this," Mom said. "I don't care if we all have to band together to stop you. This is not happening."

"We'll see about that," Aunt Tillie hissed.

WELL, that was the worst dinner ever," Landon said, lifting the covers and sliding in next to me in bed a few hours later.

"You've been to dinners where poltergeists threw all the dishes against the wall," I reminded him.

"That was more fun than an entire table of deathly quiet people glaring at one another," he said. "Even the food tasted different."

"That's because my mother and aunts were angry when they made it," I said. "Their magic works differently than mine. When they feel love, it goes into whatever they're doing. That includes the food."

"Well, in that case, I always want your mother to be happy," Landon said, brushing my hair from my face so he could study me. "You know I'm going to have to get up before the sun and go to the inn, right?"

"I know."

"I can't let her leave with a thousand bottles of wine that she plans to sell illegally."

"I know."

"I'm not going to arrest her," Landon said, his eyes reflecting worry. "That's not what you're worried about, is it?"

"What makes you think I'm worried?"

"I know the way your face works," he replied. "I know when you're sad, and I know when you're happy, and I know when you're worried the second I see you."

"Maybe you're magic," I said.

"I think you're magic enough for the both of us," Landon said. "I … I'm just going to confiscate the wine. I promise."

"I know you would never arrest her," I said. "I just … do you have any idea how rough tomorrow morning is going to be? If you think Aunt Tillie is bad on a good day, wait until you try to stop her from doing something she's obviously been planning for weeks."

"It will be fine, Bay," Landon said, slipping his arm around my waist and pulling me closer until my chin could rest against his shoulder. "We're going to have a big fight, and Aunt Tillie is going to curse us with something nasty, but then we're going to have the whole day - just the two of us. Doesn't that sound fun?"

It did sound nice. "Did you set the alarm?"

"You can stay in bed when I get up tomorrow. You don't have to get up."

"It's my family," I said. "I should be there."

"It might be better if you're not."

"I'm going," I said. "Don't bother arguing."

Landon gave in. "Okay. If that's the case, then we need to get some sleep. We're going to need all the energy we can muster if we're going to take on Aunt Tillie tomorrow morning."

"Really? You just want to go to sleep?"

"Oh, well, I have one last detour I want to make before we travel to dreamland," he said, giving me a soft kiss. "I want to make sure you're tired enough to pass out. It's really for your benefit."

"I'm always glad to be your personal charity," I said, smiling.

"Be prepared for my donation." Landon made a face. "Huh, that went to a creepy place I wasn't really expecting."

"Shut up and kiss me," I ordered. "Morning is going to come before either one of us is ready to deal with it."

"Yes, ma'am."

The first bed was too hard. The second bed was too soft. The third bed was just right. What's the lesson here? Don't touch other people's stuff or you risk getting eaten by bears.

– Aunt Tillie's Wonderful World of Stories to Make Little Girls Shut Up

CHAPTER 2

I woke before the alarm clock the next morning, taking the opportunity to stretch languidly before getting a grip on my surroundings. It was still dark, no light filtered through the curtains, and my internal clock was muddled. What woke me?

I rubbed my bare feet along the sheets, pushing them to my left and searching for Landon's warm presence. I found only emptiness. I reached over with my hand, thinking he must have rolled to his other side in sleep. Just touching him would be enough to let me settle down and drift off again. There was no sign of him, though.

I propped myself up on my elbow, scanning the room. It was too dark to see anything and yet I knew Landon wasn't here. His heavy but always regular breathing couldn't lull me back to sleep because he wasn't in bed with me.

I swore under my breath, threw the covers off and swung my legs over the side of the mattress. He'd gone up to the inn without me; his worry about instigating a scene with Aunt Tillie caused him to sneak out without waking me. Part of me thought it was a sweet gesture. The other part was irritated. I wasn't a child. I could handle a fight. Heck, I'd grown up with the woman. I was used to fighting with her.

My bare feet landed on the bedroom floor, and I groped along the rug until I found my jeans, T-shirt and tennis shoes from the night before. I'm not much of a housekeeper. I don't generally pick up my clothes until it's time to wash them. At a time like this, my slovenly ways were a godsend.

I considered brushing my hair, knowing my mother would make a stink if she saw it disheveled, but I was too annoyed to care. I don't like fighting with Landon, but I could feel a big one brewing. It's one thing to try to protect me. It's quite another to take charge. I hate that about him. I love the man dearly, but he often falls into that trap of having to be right. Of course, since I have trouble being wrong, we're quite the couple.

I moved around the end of the bed, smacking my shin into something hard, causing me to inadvertently cry out. "What the … ?"

I aimlessly felt around, my hands running over a hard surface that I recognized as a trunk. The only problem with that realization is that there's no trunk at the end of my bed. There's nothing. Had someone moved furniture in the middle of the night and not told me?

I carefully shuffled across the bedroom floor, slowly extending my feet like antennae in hope I wouldn't run into another piece of errant furniture that wasn't supposed to be there. When my outstretched hand hit the wall, I started feeling around for the light switch. After a few seconds of searching, I gave up. Did someone move that, too?

I pushed open the bedroom door and stepped into the living room, pulling up short and letting my eyes adjust to the brightness. Once they did, I wanted to turn around and go back into the bedroom. I'd walked out into a living room – but not my living room.

"I … ." I didn't even know what to say. What do you say when you go to sleep in your own bedroom, your smoking hot boyfriend at your side, and wake up a few hours later alone in a strange house?

My gaze bounced across the room, confusion and dread braiding to pool heavily in my stomach. I was in a cabin. Well it looked like a cabin. Without seeing the outside of the building there was no sure way to tell.

Other than the bedroom, which I'd just exited, the cabin consisted of one room. The fireplace on the far side was roaring, an iron pot of

... something ... steaming above the flames. The sofa appeared to be made out of sawed and split logs, but there were no pillows or cushions to offer comfortable seating. On the other side of the room stood a wooden counter, three bowls placed neatly atop it. That was it. There was nothing else in the room.

"This has to be a dream."

No one answered me. There was no one there to answer. I strode back to the bedroom door and threw it open, narrowing my eyes so I could stare inside. Without a better light source it was hard to make out, but it looked as though there were three beds in the room, including the one I woke up in.

I ran my hands down my clothes, breathing a sigh of relief when I recognized them. They were my jeans, T-shirt and tennis shoes. I wasn't wearing someone else's clothes. What's going on here?

For lack of something better to do, I pinched my forearm. The pain shot through me quickly, and it was enough to tell me this wasn't a dream. Well, mostly. You can't feel pain in dreams, right?

I opened my mouth to call out, Landon's name on the tip of my tongue, but I swallowed the urge when the door of the cabin swung open and three ... Oh, holy crap, this has to be a dream. There's no way I saw what I thought I saw.

"Oh, I see our guest has finally awakened. How did you sleep, my dear?"

I'd always been taught that it's polite to answer a question when it's asked of you. Of course, I've never had the opportunity to talk to a bear. That's right, a bear. There, standing in the doorway of the tiny cabin, was not one but three of them. They stood on their hind legs, their faces curious, and they stared at me as though I was the anomaly.

"I ... um ... I think I'm dreaming."

"You're not dreaming," the first bear said. "I think I would know if you were dreaming."

"Uh-huh."

The second bear, the one with the darker coat and bigger snout, pushed past the first bear and ambled in my direction. Instinct took over and I jumped back. "Don't bite me."

"We don't usually bite people," the bear said in a gravelly, male-sounding voice. "That's considered bad manners."

"Oh, well, that's good," I said, fearfully scanning the cabin. "I … how did I get here?"

"You let yourself in," the first bear said. If the second bear's voice sounded male, this one definitely sounded female. "You were tired, and you needed a place to sleep."

"First you tried my bed," the male bear said. "You said it was too hard."

"Then you tried my bed," the female bear said. "You said it was too soft."

The third and smallest bear finally decided to speak. "And then you tried my bed and declared it perfect," the bear said. The tinny tone of the voice made it hard to ascertain whether it was male or female. "That meant I had to sleep on the floor. In my own home. Thanks for that, by the way." I couldn't tell whether it was a boy or a girl, but it definitely sounded like a petulant teenager.

"Sebastian, there's no reason to be rude," the male bear said. "The girl was exhausted. She needed her sleep."

"Maybe I was exhausted, too," Sebastian said. "Did you ever think about that?"

"Not particularly," the male bear said. He turned his attention back to me. "Are you hungry?"

I couldn't eat if someone put a plate of my favorite cookies in front of me and told me they were calorie-free. "I'm good."

The female bear urged Sebastian away from the door and used her shoulder to push it shut. Since she was a bear, her expression was impossible to read. "So, do you want to tell us how you got here?"

"I have no idea," I said. "I'm still convinced this is a dream."

"It's not," she said. "Trust me."

"See, um, I can't really trust you because you're a talking bear," I said.

"I don't understand what me being a bear has to do with my trustworthiness," she replied.

"Mrs. Bear, the thing is, where I come from bears don't talk," I said.

"My name is Sheila, and I'm confused," she said. "If bears don't talk where you're from, how do you communicate with them?"

"I generally just run," I said, "although, to be fair, I've never seen a bear anywhere but in a zoo. Some people claim there have been some in the woods that surround our house, but I've never seen one. I honestly think Aunt Tillie would frighten bears so they stay away.

"My cousin Thistle says people are really seeing Bigfoot," I continued, rambling. "I don't know what to think. I mean, I went to bed last night with my boyfriend and I woke up in a cabin that belongs to a bunch of talking bears."

"I told you she was crazy," the male bear said. "Didn't I tell you? Only a crazy person would let themselves into a stranger's home and try out all the beds in the house."

"Craig, please," Sheila said. "You're upsetting the girl."

"I'm upsetting her?" If bears can look irritated, Craig was doing a mighty fine job. "She's upsetting me."

"And me," Sebastian chimed in.

I rubbed the heel of my hand against my forehead, my heart pounding as I tried to ascertain exactly what was happening. "You said that I let myself into your cabin last night and … tried out all your beds," I said. "That's what you said, right?"

Sheila nodded.

"Did I say anything?"

"You said you were tired and needed the perfect bed," Craig said.

"I have no memory of that," I said.

"I'll bet it's drugs," Sebastian said. "She looks like a pothead."

"Hey!"

"I think she's just confused," Sheila said. "Maybe she got hit on the head or something."

My hand flew up and checked my head, going over the entire expanse twice to see whether I could detect a bump or open wound.

There was nothing. Crap. "And we're entirely sure I'm not dreaming, right?"

"Why do you keep thinking you're dreaming?" Craig asked.

"Because you're bears ... and you're talking ... and I didn't fall asleep wherever this is," I replied. "Where is this, by the way?"

"It's the woods," Sheila said.

"What woods?"

"Just ... the woods."

"There's no name for the woods?" I pressed.

"What woods have names?"

"I have no idea," I said. "I just ... I really want to wake up right now. You're not supposed to fear passing out when you're dreaming. That doesn't happen. Oh, and Sherwood Forest is a wooded area that's named."

"You're not dreaming, pothead," Sebastian said. "I can't believe we let a pothead into our house. This is so wrong. All I've heard for the past two years is how bad drugs are, and now we have a druggie in our house. This is a great way to set an example."

"I am not a druggie," I snapped. Wait, how do bears know about pot? "I'm just ... confused."

"This bites the big one," Sebastian said, throwing himself dramatically on the wooden sofa. "If we're going to have a human guest, it should at least be someone fun ... like Kim Kardashian."

I think I was just insulted. "I don't want to be here any more than you want me to be here, kid," I said. "I'm just as confused as you are."

"Then go," Sebastian said.

"Sebastian, stop being rude," Sheila said. "We can't kick the girl out when she's so clearly ... unbalanced."

"I'm not unbalanced," I said. "I'm trying to get a handle on all of this. There's something ... off."

"Of course there's something off," Sebastian said. "You came into our house and slept in all of our beds. You're crazy."

"This is a fairy tale," I countered.

"There aren't any fairies here," Sheila said. "You don't see fairies, do you? Because, if you do, I'm going to start wondering if my son is right. You very well may be a pothead."

"I'm not a pothead," I said. "I don't see fairies. I said this was a fairy tale. There's a difference."

"What's a fairy tale?" Sebastian asked, interested. "Are they actual tails of fairies? Can you eat them?"

"I … ." This was the most surreal conversation I'd ever had and I once spent a drunken Sunday afternoon debating what kind of broom Aunt Tillie would fly if she were a fictional witch. "I don't know what to do."

"I think you need something to eat," Sheila said. "If you get something in your stomach you'll feel better."

"We caught some fish while we were out," Craig said. "Do you like fish?"

The thought of food made me want to vomit. That would probably send the wrong message to my … hosts. "I'm not hungry."

"You need to eat," Craig said. "You're very pale, and your fur looks … uneven."

"It's not fur," I said. "It's hair. It's not uneven. Well, it is. It's just bedhead, though."

"If you say so," Sebastian said. He then mime coughed "freak" as he glanced over his shoulder.

"Listen, thank you so much for your hospitality," I said, "but I think I need to be on my way."

"Where are you going to go?" Sheila asked.

"I don't have any idea," I said. "I just know there are no answers for me here."

"Are you expecting answers?" Craig asked. "You might find a whole lot more than answers if you go wandering around the woods without any idea where you're heading."

I worried that was true. "I still think this is a dream," I said. "If it is a dream, I'm obviously meant to work something out before the dream ends. I don't think that something is here."

"Well, if you're sure," Sheila said. "Just keep in mind, you might not be able to find your way back."

"I guess that's a chance I'll have to take," I said.

After a few more minutes of arguing, Sheila and Craig bid me reluctant farewells while Sebastian growled occasional insults in my direction. I walked out of the cabin with nothing but the clothes on my back and fear weighing my shoulders down.

This had to be a dream. There was no other explanation. What else could be going on here?

I was halfway down the gravel walkway in front of the cabin when I heard the sound of heavy feet in the trees next to me. I jumped when a figure bolted through the underbrush, relief washing over me when I recognized a familiar silhouette. "Landon?"

He swiveled quickly, his gaze landing on me. "Bay?"

I threw myself into his arms, not caring in the least that I was dreaming. All I cared was that he hadn't slipped out of bed and left me alone after all. He hadn't abandoned me. "I've never been so happy to see someone in my entire life."

The road less traveled may be more exciting, but it's also probably not paved. If it's not paved, that means there are snakes. If there are snakes, they're going to bite you. If you get bitten, you're going to cry. If you cry, don't come running to me. I can't stand it when you cry. It gives me a headache.

– Aunt Tillie's Wonderful World of Stories to Make Little Girls Shut Up

CHAPTER 3

"What is going on here?"

Landon moved to separate from me but I fought the effort and pulled him closer. "Not yet."

"Not yet what?" He wrapped his arms around me again, pulling me close and rubbing my back for a moment. "What's wrong?"

"I just ... I had the strangest thing happen to me," I murmured, burying my face in the hollow between Landon's shoulder and neck.

Landon ran his hand down the back of my head one more time and gave me a quick kiss on the forehead before forcing me far enough away that he could see my face. "You don't know about weird."

"Really? I woke up in bed alone. I thought you'd left me there and gone to the inn to face off with Aunt Tillie on your own. I was really angry, by the way. Don't ever do that."

Landon rolled his eyes. "First, I said I was going to wake you up," he said. "I do what I say. I had every intention of waking you up. But I didn't wake up in your bed either, in case you hadn't noticed."

I worried my bottom lip with my teeth. "I know. It's just that you're always there when I wake up. You never leave without saying goodbye, even when you have to leave early for work. I thought ... I don't know what I thought."

"Really, you're going to pick now to go all ... girl ... on me?" Landon's face was unreadable.

"I ... ."

"Good grief, Bay." He cupped the back of my head and forced my blue eyes up to his. "I would never abandon you like that. Get some perspective. We're in a very ... freaky ... place."

"I know you would never abandon me," I said. Except he had once, I added, internally. He had walked away once.

Landon narrowed his eyes, as if reading my mind. "I'll never do it again. I was confused when you told me the truth about being a witch. I'd never even imagined anything like what I saw that day. I regretted it the second I did it."

"I know," I said. "I didn't say anything."

"I saw it in your face," he said. "I can't keep apologizing for what I did."

"I didn't mean to bring that up now," I said. "I have no idea why I did it. It just popped in my head. I'm sorry."

"Don't be sorry," Landon said. "We can talk about this if you want to. We just can't talk about it now."

I knew he was right. "Okay."

"Okay," Landon said, leaning forward so he could give me another kiss. "Tell me what happened after you woke up."

"Well, I walked out of what I thought was my bedroom and found myself in a cabin," I said. "It was really cute. Rustic. It had this wooden furniture that would be really adorable with cushions."

"Thanks for the interior decorating commentary, sweetie," Landon said. "Then what happened?"

"Well, the door opened, and three ... bears ... walked into the cabin."

Landon's eyebrows shot up. "Bears?"

"Bears," I confirmed. "Oh, and they could talk."

"Talk?"

"Their names were Craig, Sheila and Sebastian," I said. "They claimed I walked into their cabin last night and tried to sleep in all of their beds."

"You tried to ... have sex with the bears?" Landon looked appalled.

"No! You have a filthy mind. They had three beds. They said I tried them all out, claiming one was too hard, one was too soft, and one was ... just right."

"Like the fairy tale," Landon mused, rubbing his hands over my shoulders absent-mindedly.

"Yes. This is a dream, right?"

"I don't know," Landon said. "Can two people share the same dream?"

I shrugged, lost. "Where did you wake up?"

Landon scowled. "I woke up on a beach," he said. "I was convinced it was a dream, just like you. It was dark, and I could hear water lapping the shoreline, and it really made me have to go to the bathroom.

"So, I kind of rolled over," he continued. "I reached for you. I expected to find you in the bed next to me. It was as though I was in that hazy spot between sleep and consciousness. You weren't there, though."

I slipped a little closer to him. "Did you think I left you in bed alone?"

"I thought you were in the bathroom or something," Landon said. "When I felt for you, though, I realized it wasn't a bed. I was on sand and, quite frankly, it was in my ... underwear."

I fought the urge to laugh. He was so serious. Just being reunited with him was enough to make me smile, though. "Is it still in your underwear?"

"Don't try to distract me, Bay."

"Sorry."

"Then I heard something ... splashing ... in the water," Landon said. "It took me a few minutes to realize I wasn't dreaming. Or, to be more accurate, I still thought I was dreaming but I decided to go with the flow thinking I would eventually wake up."

"That's what I did, too."

"Do you want me to high-five you?"

He was grumpy. I guess I couldn't blame him. "Tell me what happened."

"I kept hearing the splashing," Landon said. "I rolled over, and do you know what I saw?"

"Water?"

"You're cute, sweetie, but I can only take so much right now," Landon warned.

"You asked a question. I answered it." Now I was starting to feel crabby, too.

"I'm sorry," Landon said, holding his hands up. "I just ... we're stuck in a dream together, Bay. We're stuck in a dream together. You shared a cabin with bears and I ... well ... I woke up by an ocean."

"You said you heard splashing," I said. "What was it?"

"I ... ." He was conflicted, as though he didn't want to tell me what happened.

"Landon, you're going to have to tell me if you want us to figure this out," I said.

He pressed his lips together, averting his eyes.

"What did you see?"

"You're going to think I'm crazy."

"I just told you I saw three talking bears and you didn't call me a liar once," I said. "I think I'm ready to believe anything you have to tell me."

"There was a ... woman ... in the water," Landon said.

"A woman?"

He nodded.

"What kind of woman?"

"The naked kind."

My heart dropped. "Did you ... do something with the naked woman?"

"Of course not," Landon snapped.

"It's a dream," I said. "Sometimes people do stuff in dreams that they wouldn't do in real life."

"Who are you hanging out with in your dreams?"

I balked. "No one."

"We're going to talk about this later," he warned. "I didn't do anything with her. She was naked ... and she ... um ... had a tail."

"A tail?"

"She was a mermaid," Landon said, finally gritting the words out. "Does that make you happy? She was a mermaid."

"Oh, man, are you kidding me?"

Landon shook his head, pinching the bridge of his nose as though trying to ward off the world's biggest headache. "She kept splashing and singing in this ... horrific ... voice."

"It's like *The Little Mermaid*," I said. "Another fairy tale."

"I thought that mermaid was supposed to have a beautiful voice?"

"She is," I said, thoughtful. "Did the mermaid have red hair?"

Landon nodded.

"Was she alone?"

"As far as I could tell."

"No singing crustaceans or big sea hags hanging around, right?"

"No. Just the naked mermaid. And she was ... um ... making suggestive comments."

I laughed. I couldn't help myself. "Are you saying the naked mermaid was hitting on you?"

"Yes. I didn't touch her, though! All I could think about was you."

"This is just so ... odd."

"What was your first clue?" Landon asked, bewildered. "Was it the talking bears or the vulgar mermaid?"

"How did you end things with the mermaid?"

"She kept asking me whether I wanted to see her seashell," Landon said, tilting his head to the side. "I didn't, so I said my goodbyes and then I took off into the woods."

"Then what happened?"

"I don't know," he said. "I just kept walking. I had no idea where I was going. There was no light. I just ... for some reason I knew to come in this direction. It was as if I felt you."

"You knew I was here?"

"No. I knew I had to come in this direction. Until I actually saw you I didn't know you were here with me. I thought you were home. I thought you were safe in your bed. I thought we were both safe in your bed and we were going to wake up any moment."

"Do you still think we're dreaming?" I asked.

"Do you?"

I was starting to have my doubts. Still, there was no other rational explanation. "I don't know how we could be sharing the same dream."

"Could it be magic?"

"I'm not familiar with a lot of dream magic," I said. "We don't believe in using it."

"What is dream magic, and why don't you use it?"

I sighed. "Most people believe that your dreams are nothing more than your subconscious' way of working out your day or the problems you're grappling with while you're awake," I said. "There are some who believe your dreams are more."

Landon waited, silent.

"Some people believe your dreams are wishes that can come true if you go after them," I said. "Those people believe that … if you mess with someone's dream and change the outcome … you're tempting fate."

"Are you saying that messing with someone's dream could affect their life?"

"Some people believe that," I said.

"You keep saying 'some people.' What do you believe?"

"I believe that dreams are just dreams," I said. "I also believe that interrupting dreams can have a negative impact on people's lives. I don't think destroying a dream destroys a life, if that's what you expect me to say.

"I do think that destroying a dream can make someone sad, though," I continued. "When I was a kid, all I had were dreams. I didn't have a happy reality, so I always escaped into dreams. I would have hated for someone to ruin that for me."

Landon's face softened. "Come here." He pulled me in for a hug. "You can't say stuff like that and not expect me to hug you."

I rested my face against his shoulder. "I'm not sure this is a dream."

"If it's not a dream, what is it?"

I shrugged. "I have no idea. The thing is, this could be a dream ... as long as it's just my dream. Maybe you're a figment of my imagination. Maybe I conjured you into my dream because I needed you."

"That doesn't explain how I'm aware of what's going on," Landon pointed out.

"I know," I said. "I just don't think we could be sharing the same dream."

Landon rubbed his hand over his chin, thoughtful. "Could it be a spell?"

That was a very good question. "If it's not a dream, it has to be a spell."

"Who would have cast it?"

"Well, my first guess is Aunt Tillie," I said. "No one else has a reason to cast a spell on us."

"Do you think this is a way for her to distract us so she can sell her wine without repercussions?"

"It's possible. It's just ... ."

"What?"

"We're not the only ones standing in her way," I said. "She would have to curse Thistle, Clove, Mom, Marnie and Twila, too."

"Do you think they're all here?"

I shrugged. "I don't know. She could have cursed us all into our own different fairy tale worlds. I just don't know."

"Go with your gut, sweetie," Landon said. "If this is a spell, what do we have to do to break it?"

"It's either going to run its course because Aunt Tillie put a time limit on it or we're going to have to solve the puzzle to get out ourselves," I said.

"What puzzle?"

"I don't know," I admitted. "There's something so familiar about this. I can't put my finger on it."

"It's fairy tales," Landon said. "Your mother probably read them to you all the time when you were a kid."

"She did. Marnie and Twila did, too. This is ... different."

"How?"

"I don't know," I said. "It's just not ... the same as I remember from when I was a kid."

"What do you want to do?" Landon asked. "Do you want to find a spot to hunker down in and wait for this to end or do you want to go looking to see whether anyone else is here?"

I thought about it for a moment. "I think we should work our way through the story," I said. "If we wait, and there is no time limit, we're burning time. At least this way we'll be doing something."

"Okay," Landon said, pressing another kiss to my forehead and linking his fingers with mine. "I'd rather be proactive, too. Which way?"

"Why are you asking me?"

"You're magic, sweetie," Landon said. "I mean that in more ways than one. You're the one who is going to lead us out of this."

I bit my lip, warmth washing over me. He always knew the best way to make me feel better. I glanced around, debating which direction to head in, and then pointed. "That way."

"That's as good a way as any," Landon said. "Can I ask why you picked it?"

"I just feel we need to go that way."

Landon smiled. "Then let's go. I just hope the next fairy tale monstrosity can sing. There's nothing worse than a tone-deaf mermaid with a vulgar tongue and sexual ... issues."

I smirked. "Are you scarred for life?"

"Let's just say I'm never going to be able to watch that movie again without having a flashback and leave it at that," he said, tugging my hand. "Come on. If we're lucky, we'll be able to find some reinforcements. More minds can only mean more ideas on how to get us out of this."

"You realize more minds is going to mean more complaining, too, right?"

"Oh, I know," Landon said. "Since I'm a never-ending fount of complaints right now, though, I can take it. Misery loves company, right?"

"I just know I love you right now," I said.

"Right back at you. Now, come on. These woods are starting to give me the creeps."

There are many different kinds of princesses. Some of them need a prince to save them. The best ones, though, save themselves. Always be the second kind of princess. You don't need anyone else to save you – unless they have pie. If they have pie, go ahead and let them save you. You can always save yourself down the road. You might not find another decent pie for days.

– Aunt Tillie's Wonderful World of Stories to Make Little Girls Shut Up

CHAPTER 4

"Do you think it's going to remain night the whole time we're here, or are we eventually going to see daylight?" Landon asked.

We walked the narrow pathway together, our hands clasped and shoulders occasionally touching. Neither one of us felt comfortable enough to wander too far from the one landmark we had. It was as though we both worried that separating would somehow zip one of us into separate fairy tales.

"I don't know," I said. "The good news is that the moon is really bright, so it's lighting things relatively well. Do you miss the sun already?"

"I don't care about the sun as much as I do about the light," Landon said. "If it was light out I wouldn't constantly be looking over my shoulder and searching the shadows for something trying to attack us. This place makes me ... uneasy."

I finally realized one of the reasons he was so uncomfortable. "You don't have a weapon. You feel naked without it."

He shook his head, his expression rueful. "Do you think less of me because I want to take a gun to a fairy tale fight?"

"Nothing could ever make me think less of you," I said, gripping his hand tightly. "I love you regardless. Well, that's not entirely true. If you ever tell me you have a clown fetish it's over."

"You're so cute I can't stand it sometimes," Landon said. His face sobered. "There aren't any clowns in fairy tales, right?"

I shook my head. "Not that I remember."

"Good," Landon said. "I can take talking bears and nymphomaniac mermaids. I can't take clowns, though."

"I didn't know you were coulrophobic."

"I have no idea what that is," Landon said. "If it's gross, I'm going to deny having it, though."

"It's a fear of clowns," I said. "It's a pretty common fear."

"I didn't say I was afraid of them," Landon said. "I said I didn't like them."

"Because you're afraid of them."

"I'm not afraid of them."

"There's nothing to be embarrassed about," I said. "I'm afraid of spiders."

"Whatever," Landon said, rolling his eyes. "I'm not afraid of clowns."

"I believe you."

"I'm not."

"I didn't say you were."

We were silent a few minutes, both of us scanning the foliage as we moved forward. We'd gone a long time without any surprises. That naturally meant we were about to encounter one. I don't know how I knew that. I just did.

When Landon opened his mouth again, he didn't say what I was expecting. "I'm not afraid of clowns."

I sighed. "I'm sorry I said it. I didn't mean it. I was obviously mistaken."

"You were."

"Great."

More silence.

"Bay?"

"What?" I was starting to tire.

"I don't like their big shoes and white faces," he said. "It's unnatural for a grown man to wear a rubber ball on his nose and make balloon animals. I read Stephen King's *It* when I was a kid and it scared the crap out of me."

I pursed my lips to keep from laughing. "I felt the same way about *Salem's Lot*," I admitted. "I always thought there were vampires scratching at the window, trying to get in."

"You're not going to tell anyone, right?"

"It will be our little secret."

We lapsed into silence again. The fact that he'd admitted a fear bolstered me, and I had no idea why. It was as if he was letting me see deeper inside of him. He trusted me with something he couldn't admit to anyone else. I was about to tell him what I was thinking when the sound of bitter complaining assailed my ears.

I tilted my head to the side, listening.

"This is absolutely the dumbest thing that has ever happened to me. If there were a list of dumb things in the world, this would be right on the top. It would be right next to Crocs and Snuggies."

Landon and I exchanged a look. "Thistle," we said in unison.

Landon kept steady hold of my hand as we stepped off the path and started wading through the heavy underbrush. After about two minutes of walking, the trees gave way and we found ourselves in an open area, looking out on a small pond. In the middle of that pond, standing on a huge rock with her hands on her hips, was Thistle. Unlike Landon and me, who had been able to keep access to our regular clothing, Thistle was dressed in a monstrous pink dress and had a tiara on her head.

I laughed. I couldn't help myself. "Nice dress."

Thistle snapped her head up, her usually pink hair now a dull shade of brown. She looked like a different person. "Thank the Goddess," she said. "Where have you been?"

"I've been hanging out with three bears," I said. "They had a beautiful little cabin, kind of an enhanced shed more than anything else. Oh, and they could talk."

Thistle furrowed her forehead, and even from fifty feet away – and an expanse of water separating us – I could see her mind working. "They could talk? Did they say anything interesting?"

"The kid bear thought I was a pothead," I said. "Apparently I let myself into their cabin and tried to sleep in all of their beds."

"Are you suddenly a dream slut?" Thistle asked. "Are you making time with talking bears?"

Landon scowled. "Stop being … you."

"You stop being you," Thistle shot back. "Why are you two in your regular clothes? Why do you get to wear what you want and I'm in … this?"

"I'm guessing you're stuck in it until you play this particular story out," I said.

"What story?"

"We're going through fairy tales," I said.

"Aunt Tillie," Thistle grumbled. "I'm going to pop her like a zit. I'm going to …." Thistle mimed a violent act, almost losing her balance and tumbling into the water. "I'm going to make that old lady pay!"

"We have to get out of here first," I said.

"I don't even know what this is," Thistle said. "Where are we? Are we dreaming?"

"I have no idea," I said. "I don't know how all three of us could be sharing the same dream. Even Aunt Tillie wouldn't mess with dream magic."

Thistle rubbed her forehead. "You're right. She's mean, petty and bitter … and I'm going to burn her greenhouse to the ground when I get out of here … but she wouldn't mess with dream magic. That means this is something else. I kind of figured that out already."

"It also means all of us might be in here," I said.

"You've only found each other?"

"And now you," I said.

Thistle sighed dramatically. "Well, this is just great. What are we supposed to do now? Are we supposed to wander around fairy tale land until we find everyone?"

"I have no idea," I said. "We could all be in the same place, or we could be split between separate places. I just don't know."

"I think the first thing we need to do is get you off the rock," Landon said. "Why don't you jump in and swim over here? It's not that far. The dress will dry after a little bit."

"Oh, thank you," Thistle said. "I never would have thought of that myself."

"Then why are you still on the rock?" Landon asked, nonplussed.

"There's something in the water," Thistle said.

"What?"

"I don't know. I've seen a ... tail ... a couple of times."

"What kind of tail?"

"A green, scaly one," Thistle said. "It's big. That means whatever is in the water is big."

"Have you seen any teeth?"

"No. Every time I decide I'm going to risk a swim I see the tail. Then I see a big freaking turtle staring at me. Oh, and can you hear that frog croaking? It's driving me crazy. I'm going to kill it and cook it."

I ran her diatribe through my head. What fairy tale was this? "What turtle? I don't see a turtle."

"Just watch," Thistle instructed. She moved to the edge of the rock and dipped her toe into the water. The second she did something splashed a few feet away, a long tail rising out of the water and slapping back down loudly.

"That was creepy," I said.

"Wait."

Out of the corner of my eye I saw movement on the far side of the pond. I peered into the darkness, squinting until I realized what I saw. It was a shell – a large one at that. It was two feet long and three feet wide. The turtle didn't raise its head until it was next to the rock, and then it focused on Thistle as it floated there.

"I have no idea what I'm supposed to do with this," Thistle said.

"You're supposed to step on it," Landon said.

I glanced at him, surprised. "How do you know that?"

"It's the answer to the riddle," he said. "This story is about trust.

Thistle has to trust the turtle to get her over to us without dropping her in the water and feeding her to that ... thing."

"What if it doesn't work?" I asked.

"I don't see where we have much of a choice," Landon said. "You can't stay on that rock, and you can't risk swimming. You have to trust the turtle. Wow. There's something I never thought I would say."

"What happens if I fall in?" Thistle asked.

"Then swim really quickly."

"What happens if the turtle sinks?"

"Then swim really quickly."

"What happens ... ?"

"Thistle, get your butt on that turtle," Landon ordered. "We're wasting time here. We need you on this shore with us. This is the only way."

"If I get eaten, I'm going to haunt you forever," Thistle warned.

"Duly noted. Now, get on the turtle."

Landon tightened his hand around mine as we watched Thistle carefully step away from the rock. She tested the turtle with one foot before committing fully and dragging her other foot over. The second she was settled, the turtle started drifting in our direction.

The tail snapped angrily next to the rock. No head emerged, though, and there was no sign of the water marauder following the turtle. Thistle was on the shore within seconds. Her face flushed when she felt the solid ground beneath her, and she raced to me so she could give me a hug. I think she needed the human contact, because she's not known as a big hugger.

"Holy crap," she said. "That was so ... surreal."

"Try talking to bears," I said.

"Try having a naughty mermaid ask you if you want to see her seashell," Landon added.

Thistle laughed, the sound harsh. "Seriously?"

"Seriously," Landon said. "I woke up on a beach and Bay woke up in a strange bed."

"I still don't understand why I'm in this dress," Thistle said. "It's ... ugly."

"I would think, once this fairy tale is over, you would go back to your regular clothes," I said. "I thought the dress was part of the fairy tale."

"Maybe it still is," Landon suggested.

"Meaning?"

"Maybe this story isn't over."

"What's left?" I asked. "She got off the rock. She's safe. She passed the trust exercise."

"I have no idea," Landon said. "If I could explain this freaky place I would."

A loud croak caused the three of us to jump, our gazes shifting to a large bullfrog perched on a rock a few feet away. It looked like a normal frog other than the fact that it stared at us.

"Do you think it can talk?" I asked.

"The turtle and the water monster couldn't," Thistle said. "I tried. Trust me. I was standing on that rock for about two hours and I tried talking to both of them because I was desperate."

"Hi, frog," I said, smiling down at it. "Can you talk?"

The frog croaked again.

"I guess not, huh?"

Another croak.

"What do you want to do?" I asked. "Do you want to stick around and see whether there's more to the fairy tale so you can get rid of that dress or do you want to move on?"

"I don't understand what this is," Thistle said. "When I first woke up, I was sure I was dreaming."

"Join the club," Landon said.

"It didn't take me long to realize it wasn't a dream, though," Thistle said. "Or, to be more precise, it didn't take me long to realize it wasn't a normal dream."

"How did you figure it out?" I asked. "I talked to the bears for ten minutes before I came to the same conclusion."

"The water kept splashing on me," Thistle said. "When you're in a dream, even if you're swimming, you don't feel the water. You just know you're swimming. I could feel every drop as it landed on me."

"Landon could feel the sand in his underwear," I said. "That was his first clue that this was more than your normal dream."

"You have sand in your underwear?" Thistle asked. "Does it chafe?"

"Wouldn't you like to know?"

"Not really," Thistle said.

The frog croaked again and then slapped its foot against the rock. I glanced back at the frog. "Does anyone else think the frog might mean something?"

"It's fairy tales," Landon said. "The frog means something. But we have to figure out what. What fairy tales have frogs?"

"I can only think of the one where the princess is supposed to kiss the frog," I said. I turned my attention back to Thistle. "Maybe you're supposed to kiss the frog."

"Over my dead body," Thistle snapped. "I already had to ride a turtle. I am not kissing a frog. That's just … gross."

"I think that's why you're wearing the dress," I said. "You're the princess."

"Well, I'm not going to do it," Thistle said. "You do it."

"I'm not wearing the dress."

"We can trade clothes."

"Yeah, that's not happening," I said.

"Besides, this is your fairy tale," Landon said. "Bay woke up with the bears because that was her fairy tale. I woke up with the creepy mermaid because that was my fairy tale. This is still your fairy tale."

"Well, I'm not finishing it then," Thistle said. "I'd rather walk ten miles in this dress than kiss a frog. I'm just not going to do it."

"Then let's get going," Landon said. "There's no reason for us to hang around here any longer."

The frog croaked again, and this time the sound was almost pitiful.

"I'm sorry," Landon said. "It doesn't look like you're going to get any action today, my friend. I think you hung your legs on the wrong princess. This one is a little grumpy."

Another croak.

"Let's go," Thistle said. "Which way?"

Landon looked to me for an answer. I pressed my eyes shut again, concentrating. "That way." I pointed.

"How can you know?" Thistle asked.

I shrugged. "I don't know. This is how we found you, though."

Thistle shrugged. "Okay. Let's see what new horror we find. I have a feeling this is going to be the longest night ever."

I couldn't help but agree, and that was disconcerting.

If you're going to risk disfigurement by lying, the moral of the story is to make sure it's a good lie and it's worth it. If you're going to look like a freak for the rest of your life, you'd better get something really good out of the situation – like money, or a convertible or a snowplow.

– Aunt Tillie's Wonderful World of Stories to Make Little Girls Shut Up

CHAPTER 5

"How long do you think we're going to be stuck here?" Thistle asked.

We walked along the pathway, our eyes busy as we looked for the next fairy tale catastrophe. Thistle's pink dress made odd crinkling noises as she moved. It was starting to grate, but no one wanted to comment on it. We were already in a precarious situation; adding a fight to the mix wasn't going to do anyone any good.

"I don't know," I said. "It depends on whether this is a timed curse or whether we have to actually work our way through the entire world to get out."

"It's like a video game," Landon said.

"What's like a video game?"

"This ... all of it," he said, gesturing animatedly. "We keep finding new tasks to accomplish. We can't win unless we finish all the tasks. We can't leave until we win. It's a video game."

"Do you think we're earning points?" Thistle asked.

Landon shrugged. "I don't know. Does Aunt Tillie play a lot of video games?"

"Just *Candy Crush* and *Bubble Witch Saga*," I said. "She likes the first one because she likes candy and she likes the second one because ... ."

"She's a witch," Landon finished. "I get it."

"No, she likes the second one because she likes to fire at things and knock them down," I said. "She doesn't like the witch in it. She doesn't think it looks realistic."

Landon snorted. "She never ceases to amaze me."

"I thought you said that about me?"

"You, too." Landon shifted his attention to Thistle. "Are you worried Marcus is here somewhere?"

"I don't know," Thistle said. "I can see why she cursed you in here with us. You were trying to stop her. You had the power to stop her. Marcus always helps her. She might not have cursed him. She really likes him."

"I can see that," I said. "I definitely think Clove is in here, though."

"Me, too," Thistle said. "That means she's on her own somewhere."

"What fairy tale do you think she's in?"

"I have no idea," Thistle said. "I … do you hear that?"

"What?"

"There's something in the bushes."

We stopped moving, but even as she shifted only her shoulders Thistle's dress made noise.

"Thistle, stop moving," Landon ordered.

"I'm looking to see where the noise is coming from," Thistle argued.

"The noise is coming from that ugly dress," Landon said. "Stand still."

"You can't tell me what to do."

"I'm going to tie you to a tree and leave you here if you don't shut up and stop moving," Landon shot back.

"You don't have any rope."

"This is a magic world," he said. "Maybe one will drop from the sky."

That brought up an interesting idea. "It's a magic world," I muttered, my mind busy.

"That's what I just said," Landon said, nonplussed.

"No, it's a magic world," I said. "We have magic. Do you think it works here?"

"That's a good question," Thistle said. "Let's see." She glanced around, the dress crinkling again. Every time the dress made a sound, Landon cringed as if someone raked their fingernails across a chalkboard.

Thistle focused on a nearby bush and squinted, focusing on it. She muttered a quick spell under her breath and … nothing. She tried again and got the same result.

"Our magic doesn't work," Thistle said.

"What did you try to do?"

"I tried to set the bush on fire."

"That seems like a great idea when we're trapped in a forest we can't get out of," Landon said. "Let's set it on fire and really make things uncomfortable."

"No one needs your sarcasm," Thistle said.

"I think it's completely appropriate," Landon replied.

I stepped between them, holding up my hands to earn a temporary reprieve from the sound of their voices. "Can we please not fight? This is bad enough without everyone fighting."

"I'm not the one picking a fight," Landon said.

"You've done nothing but snipe at me for the last half hour," Thistle countered. "It's not my fault you're here. In fact, if you want to get down to it, it's your fault we're here."

Uh-oh.

"My fault?" Landon arched an eyebrow. "My fault?"

"You were the one who told her you were going to confiscate her wine," Thistle said.

"I told her that selling it without a license was illegal," Landon said. "It is illegal. Your mothers were the ones really going after her this time."

"That's a good point," I said. "Not that I want them here – and I really don't because if we're fighting already we're going to kill one another if our mothers are added to this mix – but it was Mom, Marnie and Twila who were really going after her this time."

"Actually, it was just Winnie," Thistle said. "My mom is wishy-washy, and Marnie didn't look as if she really cared. It was as if she was trying to stay loyal to Winnie more than anything else."

"Hey, if I have to put up with my mother in this fairy tale world you should have to put up with yours, too," I grumbled.

"If I know Aunt Tillie, she split us up," Thistle said. "She probably cursed the three of us … and Landon … to this world and our mothers to another. She'd be running a big risk to let us all spend too much time together with nothing better to do than plot against her."

She had a point. "I think the first thing we have to do is find Clove," I said. "She's probably freaking out."

"I agree," Thistle said. "I … seriously, can't you hear that?" She turned swiftly and focused on the bushes to our left. "There's something in there."

"Are you sure?" Landon asked.

"No, I'm making it up because I want to mess with you. Of course I'm sure."

Landon scorched Thistle with a harsh look. "I have this incredible urge to gag you."

"Right back at you."

Landon slipped around me and cautiously approached the bushes. He gave the bushes as wide a berth as he dared, and I didn't miss his hand going to the spot on his waist where his gun usually rested only to find it absent. He was feeling vulnerable, I reminded myself. He didn't mean to be crabby, but he was so far out of his element he was having trouble wrapping his head around what was happening.

"All right, come out of there," Landon said.

This time not only could we hear the rustling in the bushes we could see the branches moving.

"What is it?" I asked.

"Is it a monster?" Thistle asked.

"It's not a clown, is it?" I asked.

Landon shot me a quelling look. "I'm not sure … ."

"It's me!"

We all took a step back when a dark figure jumped out of the bushes, hands raised above its head. It took us only a second to recognize the new player.

"Sam?"

"Last time I checked," Sam said. "Of course, I don't really recognize this ... outfit."

"Join the club," Thistle said, tilting her head to the side to study Sam's tiny shorts, white shirt and odd vest. I'd never seen him wear a hat before, so the yellow one with the red feather on top of his head was ... distracting. "Who are you supposed to be?"

I had a feeling I knew. "At least he's not wooden," I said. "That would be ... uncomfortable ... to deal with."

"Wooden?" Thistle wrinkled her nose. "Oh. You're Pinocchio. That's interesting. I wonder why you got shoved in that fairy tale."

"Fairy tale?" Sam asked, confused. "Is that what's going on?"

"What did you think was happening?" I asked.

"I had no idea," Sam said. "All I know is I went to bed with Clove next to me and woke up in a really weird place."

"Where?" Landon asked.

"Is that really important?" Sam asked. "If I tell you, you're going to think I'm crazy."

"Just to catch you up, you should know that I woke up with talking bears, Thistle was trapped on a rock and had to ride a turtle to get to safety and Landon ... well ... he had a sexually suggestive mermaid try to show him her seashell," I said.

Sam's eyes widened as his gaze darted between us. "Is that true?"

"Unfortunately," Landon said. "She was also tone deaf and swore like a trucker."

"That's still better than what happened to me," Sam said.

"I had to ride a turtle," Thistle said. "Look at my dress."

"At least your legs are covered," Sam said. "I look like I'm about to take my clothes off in an all-male burlesque show."

"Only if they're in to some really kinky stuff," I said. "Tell us what happened. I promise we won't laugh."

"Fine," Sam said, glancing over his shoulder to make sure no one was listening. I had no idea who he thought he was saving face for; we were all in the same boat. "When I first woke up, I was in a ... store or something."

"A store?"

"I had strings attached to my arms and I was on display in the storefront," Sam said.

"You weren't wooden, though, right?"

Sam shook his head. "I thought I was dreaming."

"We all thought we were dreaming," Landon said. "Go on."

"After a minute or so I managed to get down, and when I looked around the store I found this creepy old guy watching me," Sam said. "He had white hair, and he was wearing those really thick magnifying glasses because he was working on some craft project."

"Did he talk to you?" I asked.

"He said he'd been hoping for a son for a long time, but I wasn't what he had in mind," Sam said. "I am not going into the details about how weird he was. Suffice it to say that I don't think he wanted a child because he was dying to become a father."

"Gross," Thistle said, making a face. "That is so wrong."

Something about this story tugged on a long-forgotten memory, but I couldn't quite clear my mind enough to grasp it.

"I kind of ... bashed him over the head with a lamp and when I raced for the door I was accosted by a ... bug," Sam said. "It talked."

"Was it a cricket?" Thistle asked.

"I guess," Sam conceded. "It kept saying weird things about being brave and true. I wasn't really in a listening mood – and I couldn't find a flyswatter. I bolted from the store. I was expecting to find a town, but it was just the one store in the middle of nowhere. There was nothing else around.

"I heard the guy coming to in the store so I ran into the woods," he continued. "I hid there for as long as I could. I wanted to make sure he wasn't following me, and then I just started walking."

"How long have you been awake?" Landon asked.

"A few hours," Sam said. "I'm not sure. It's not as if I have a way to keep track of time."

"How did you find us?" Thistle asked.

"It was by accident really," Sam said. "I just kept moving in the same direction – or what I hoped was the same direction – and then I heard voices. I hid in the bush at first because I wasn't sure what to expect."

"I don't blame you," Landon said. "There's no shame in it. This place is one freak show after another. I would have hidden, too."

"You didn't hide when I saw you," I said. "You came straight toward me."

"That was after I recognized you," Landon said. "I hung back in the trees for a minute or two until I was sure it was you. I wasn't a one-hundred percent sure until you saw me and started running."

"Were you running from the bears?" Sam asked.

"Actually, other than being bears, they weren't that bad," I said. "The teenage one was a mouthy pain, but he was still pretty normal."

"Except they were talking bears," Sam said.

"They were. They said I came into their house the night before and tried out all of their beds until I found one that was just right."

"You're Goldilocks."

"Maybe," I said.

"She was the heroine in that story," Sam said.

"I don't think we're only one thing here," I said. "I think we're working our way through stories, but just because we've solved one story doesn't mean we won't have to face another. Aunt Tillie wouldn't make it that easy."

"Did she curse our dreams?" Sam asked.

Thistle and I exchanged a look. "We're not quite sure what this is yet," Thistle said. "We've never really dabbled in dream magic. We don't think Aunt Tillie would do that."

"I wasn't under the impression that she had many boundaries," Sam said.

"She doesn't," Thistle said. "The rules she believes in, though, she sticks to. She's never messed with dream magic before. I don't think she would start now."

"This is all because she didn't want Landon to confiscate her wine, right? No offense, but why are we all here? Shouldn't she be punishing only Landon?"

"Thanks, man," Landon said, irritated. "I'm glad we're all on the same side here."

I put my hand on his arm to calm him. "Landon ... ."

Landon ran his tongue over his teeth, clearly trying to tamp down his temper. "I'm sorry," he said. "It's just ... this is all so unbelievable. I can't believe this is happening. I kind of wish I'd hidden in a bush as you did. I could have sat it out until this was all over with."

"I wasn't hiding because I was afraid," Sam protested. "I was hiding because I was being cautious."

I rolled my eyes, and out of the corner of one of them saw a hint of movement on Sam's face. Was he giving me a dirty look? I turned back to him, but his face was placid. Something was different about it, though.

"What was that?" I asked.

"What was what?" Sam asked, confused.

"Your face. Something is ... different."

"Oh, great, am I starting to turn to wood?" Sam ran his fingers over his forehead and cheeks, worried. "This is my favorite night ever!"

It happened again. This time I was sure of it. While I was staring directly at him I realized what the change was. So did Thistle.

"Your nose just grew," Thistle said, pointing.

"What?" Sam clapped his hand over his nose, horrified. "My nose is getting bigger?"

"You're Pinocchio," I said. "If you lie, your nose gets bigger."

"I wasn't lying. Crap. I felt it this time." Sam was starting to panic.

"You need to stop lying," Thistle said. "Even little ones are going to affect you. If I were you, I'd keep my mouth shut as much as possible."

Sam glared at her. "Thanks for that."

"I don't know what else to tell you," Thistle said. "I don't think the curse knows the difference between truth and sarcasm, so you have to be careful."

"Maybe if we're lucky his nose will grow long enough that it can support part of your dress and it won't make noise," Landon suggested.

"Shut up!"

"Everyone shut up," I said, rubbing the crease between my eyebrows. "Stop arguing."

"No one is arguing," Landon said, rubbing my back. "We're just ... expressing ourselves in loud voices."

"We're frustrated," Sam said.

"We're all frustrated," I said. "We have a bigger worry, though."

"Which is?"

"We still haven't found Clove," I said.

Sam's face drained of color. "She's out there all alone. We have to find her."

"There's one other thing," I said.

Everyone waited.

"If Sam is here, I'm going to guess Marcus is here, too," I said.

Thistle balked. "Aunt Tillie likes Marcus, though."

"It's fairy tales, Thistle," I said, keeping my voice low. "That means there's almost always a princess and a prince."

"Crap," Thistle grumbled. "This is so unfair."

"We have to stick together," I said. "Our first order of business is finding Clove."

"What about Marcus?"

"Hopefully he'll find us," Landon said. "He can take care of himself. Don't worry about that. Bay is right, though. We need to find Clove."

"She's probably terrified," Sam said.

"Where do we start looking?" Thistle asked. "Were we heading in this direction just so we could meet up with Sam, or will we find Clove this way?"

I didn't know the answer to the question. Thankfully, I didn't have to try to scrape something up. At that exact moment, an ear-splitting scream tore through the night, and we all snapped our attention in its direction.

"Somebody help me!"

"Clove," Sam said, pushing past us and breaking into a run. "Clove!"

"Great!" Landon said. "I was worried things were about to get boring."

If your hair is long enough for someone to climb it, then it's long enough to cut off and climb down yourself. Suck it up and save yourself. Sitting around and waiting for a man is a complete and total waste of time.

– *Aunt Tillie's Wonderful World of Stories to Make Little Girls Shut Up*

CHAPTER 6

We raced through the woods, branches reaching out to scratch our faces, but nothing could stop us. We'd located our missing cousin, and it sounded as though she was in trouble.

We escaped the woods and found ourselves on an expansive and well-manicured lawn, the moon above casting an eerie pall over the area. In the center of the lawn was a high tower. The lone spire resembled a partially finished castle, and there was only one window in the stone edifice.

"Where is she?" Thistle asked, bending over to catch her breath.

"Help me!"

I glanced around, and when my gaze finally landed on the tower window I had to swallow the worry bubbling up in my throat. "Crap."

"What am I looking at?" Landon asked, worried. "Is she in that tower?"

I pointed to the window. It was high in the tower, at least fifty feet above the ground. A faint light flickered inside, and a small figure moved back and forth at the window. "She's up there."

"Is something attacking her?"

I shrugged. I had no idea.

"Clove," Sam shouted. "Are you okay?"

"Sam?" Clove's voice was broken, as if she'd been crying. "Is that really you?"

"It's me."

"What are you wearing?"

"He's Pinocchio," Thistle said, moving up to his side.

"Holy Godiva! What are you wearing?" Clove asked, giggling maniacally. "You look ... so stupid. What is that?"

"The worst Halloween costume ever," Thistle said, bitterly. "Bay and Landon woke up in their own clothes. Sam and I got stuck in this ... crap."

"Bay and Landon?" Clove sounded hopeful. "We're all here together?"

"Yes, and we're thrilled," Landon said. He scanned the side of the tower. "This is really odd construction. Where's the door?"

"There is no door," Clove said. "I've been searching for a way out for hours."

"Did you wake up there?" I asked.

"Yes. I thought I was dreaming at first."

That was beginning to be our mantra.

"Are you alone in there?" Landon asked.

"Yes."

Well, that was something at least. "And you're sure there's no door or way out?" I asked, focusing on Clove's terrified face. "How did you get in there if there's no door?"

"I just woke up here," Clove snapped. "How am I supposed to know?"

"This really isn't bringing out the best in any of us," Thistle said.

"We're all tired ... and scared," I said. I blew out a frustrated sigh. "Clove, maybe we can find something to pad the ground here and you can jump."

"Like what?" Thistle asked.

"I don't know," I shrugged. "Tree branches?"

"I am not jumping from this high up. I'll break my neck."

"She's not jumping," Sam agreed. "There has to be a ... trick ... to end this fairy tale."

Clove tilted her head to the side, confused. "Fairy tale?"

"We've been cursed into fairy tales, or childhood stories, whatever you prefer," I said. "I woke up with three talking bears. Landon played footsies with a mermaid. Thistle rode a turtle. And Sam, well, he's obviously Pinocchio – complete with a growing nose when he lies."

"Fairy tales, huh?" Clove glanced back into the room.

"I wasn't telling big lies," Sam said. "In fact, I was mostly being sarcastic."

Clove ignored him. "Aunt Tillie cursed us into fairy tales?"

"That's the theory we're running on right now," I said. "Why?"

"Oh, just, well ... ." Clove leaned down, her face disappearing from view. When she returned to the window she had something gathered in her arms. She dropped it out of the window, a long sheet of something that looked like fabric falling against the tower wall. "I guess being in a fairy tale explains this."

"What is that?" Sam asked, confused.

"It's hair," Thistle said.

"Oh, crap," I muttered. "She's Rapunzel."

The black hair was so long it almost reached the ground. It was only a few feet short.

"Huh," Landon said. "Now there's something you don't see every day."

"What are we going to do?" Sam asked.

"I have no idea," I said. "Does anyone remember how Rapunzel got out of the tower in the story?"

"I never got that story," Thistle said. "It never made sense to me. Still ... I think the prince climbs her hair into the tower to rescue her, right?"

"How does that work?" I asked. "If the prince climbs her hair, won't that strand both of them in the tower?"

"Maybe the fairy tale will end if we just get someone up there with her," Thistle said.

I shrugged. It was worth a shot. "I don't see where we have a lot of other options. Someone has to climb the tower and get to Clove."

Landon blew a loud raspberry. "I guess that means I'm climbing the tower."

Sam grabbed his arm. "You? Why are you going to climb the tower to save my girlfriend?"

"Because I'm ... stronger."

"You don't know that," Sam said. "I work out three times a week."

"I'm with the FBI," Landon reminded him. "Saving people is what I do."

I was starting to think Aunt Tillie was right about his ego being a personality defect. I cleared my throat, but both men ignored me.

"She's my girlfriend," Sam said. "If anyone is climbing that tower, it's me."

"I thought we were on a timetable here," Landon countered. "Shouldn't the one who can climb up there fastest be the one to do it?"

"She's my girlfriend," Sam said.

"So?"

"That means she's my ... princess."

Landon faltered, shifting a look in my direction. "Can you believe this?"

Actually, I couldn't. I was starting to get angry. "I agree with Sam," I said. "These are fairy tales. She's his girlfriend. That means they're supposed to solve the story together."

"Are you angry with me?" Landon knit his eyebrows together, conflicted.

"Why would I possibly be angry? That's ridiculous. Of course I'm not angry."

"If you were Pinocchio, your nose would totally be growing right now," Thistle said. "You're obviously angry."

"Shut up, Thistle," I snapped, crossing my arms over my chest. "I'm not ... angry." Hurt was more like it, but there was no way I was admitting that.

"Does someone want to tell me what's going on here?" Landon asked.

"Well, if I had to guess, your princess has her nose out of joint because you're trying to save another princess," Thistle said, smirking. "Way to go, Prince Charming. Now you don't have any princesses."

Landon shifted his gaze to me. "Is she right? Are you jealous?"

"Of course not." I averted my eyes and focused on my shoes.

"Oh, this night just keeps getting better and better," Landon grumbled, running his hand through his hair. He took a step back to clear a path to the tower for Sam. "Go nuts. Get your princess."

"Thanks so much for your permission," Sam said. "It means the world to me." He clapped his hand to his nose, frowning as it expanded again. "Seriously? This is just ... crap."

"It's a lesson to teach you to stop lying," Landon said.

"Shouldn't you be paying attention to your princess?" Sam seethed. "It seems I'm not the only one having nose issues. Thistle was right. Bay's nose is out of joint because you have to be everyone's hero."

"I am not trying to be everyone's hero," Landon said. "I am trying to keep everyone together so we can get out of here safely."

Thistle sent Landon a sarcastic thumbs-up. "Good job."

"Shut up, Thistle."

"Is someone going to climb up here and get me?" Clove asked, her patience wearing thin. "I can't stay up here much longer. I'm lonely."

"I'm coming," Sam said, shuffling toward the tower wall. "Just ... hold on." He gripped a strand of Clove hair and tugged on it. "Does that hurt?"

"I don't even feel it," Clove said.

"That's a relief," Sam muttered. He tightened his hands around the hair, braced his foot against the tower, and started to climb. He moved slowly, taking special care with his foot placement and grip. The higher he got, the slower he moved, and he started to glance down at the ground with alarming frequency.

"Are you afraid of heights?" Thistle asked.

"Of course not," Sam scoffed.

Even from twenty feet beneath him we could see his nose twitch.

"I hate this stupid fairy tale world," Sam grumbled.

He wasn't the only one. After a few minutes of watching Sam,

Landon slid his eyes in my direction. "Are you really jealous because I was going to climb up there to get Clove?"

Was I? It seemed an irrational reaction. Still … . "I don't know," I admitted. "Maybe it's this place."

Landon slung an arm over my shoulders and pulled me closer, tucking me in close. "You know you're my only princess, right? Man, there's another sentence I never thought I'd say out loud."

I rolled my eyes. "I have no idea why I'm jealous. I can't explain it. I just … am."

"You were right to say something," Landon said. "This is Sam's job."

I pursed my lips but remained silent. I could feel Thistle's stare burning into me, and I didn't want to have this discussion in front of her. As if reading my mind, Thistle shuffled a few feet away. "I'm going to check the back of the tower and make sure there are no surprises waiting for us there," she said. "You two keep talking about your … issues."

"We don't have issues," I said.

"You're having some serious issues right now," Thistle said. "Don't worry. I get it. If Marcus volunteered to be Clove's prince I would be spitting nails right now."

I'd forgotten about Marcus. "Are you worried about him?"

"Right after we get Clove out of here, we need to start looking for him," Thistle said. "I'm not worried, but I am concerned."

"He's our next priority," I said.

"Don't worry," Landon said. "We'll find him. I promise."

"I know," Thistle said. "I have … faith."

The second she said the words something happened. A sparkly mist enveloped her, descending on the pink dress. Within seconds the mist dissipated to reveal Thistle in her usual jeans and T-shirt. The look on her face was almost comical. She ran her hands up and down the shirt, a genuine smile on her face.

"Thank the Goddess," she said. "I can't tell you how happy I am to be out of that dress!"

"We're all happy you're out of that dress," Landon said. "I guess trusting the turtle to get you across the pond wasn't enough."

"You had to have faith at the same time," I said. "There are lessons built into all fairy tales. We have to figure out what they are."

"Well, you two get started on that," Thistle said. "I'm still going to check the area behind the tower. Maybe we'll get lucky. Marcus could be waiting for me right over that hill."

I watched her go, relieved things were going well for one of us. When I shifted my attention back, I found Landon studying me. "What?" I felt a little self-conscious.

"Nothing," he said. "I just ... I don't want you to be upset."

"We're trapped in a fairy tale world," I said. "I don't think I have a choice but to be upset."

"You can be upset with our circumstances, but I don't want you angry with me," Landon said. "You really are my one and only princess."

I scowled. "I know. I said I was sorry. I have no idea why I was so jealous. It was stupid."

"I think it's this place," Landon said. "It's amplifying the bad parts of our personalities. The flaws, as Aunt Tillie would say. I think that's part of the curse. If we all work together, we'd figure a way out of this too quickly. She needs us to waste as much time in here as possible. That's what all the petty bickering is."

I hadn't thought of that. "That would be like her," I said. "That makes me feel a little better. I don't generally think of myself as a jealous person – that whole Lila Stevens nonsense notwithstanding."

Landon grinned and leaned over to kiss my forehead. "You're not the only one being affected. Aunt Tillie was right. I'm bossy and I yell. Apparently I also have a hero complex."

"I like your hero complex," I said, resting my head lightly on his shoulder. "There's comfort in finding normality in a surreal world like this."

"We need to try really hard not to argue," Landon said. "I know I'm guilty of doing the opposite, but now that we know what's going on we can't let our emotions get the better of us. If we feel something coming on, we ... just need to take a step back and breathe."

"That's easier said than done," I said. "Sam is climbing Clove's hair and his nose grows every time he says anything sarcastic. That's pretty dangerous when you're in our situation."

Landon chuckled. "I think that's kind of funny."

"Why?"

"Because Sam was lying when we first met him," Landon said. "It's as though it's ... karma ... coming back."

"I thought we were over that," I said. "Sam is a good man. He put himself in danger to protect me."

"I know," Landon said. "I still find it funny."

"Is that another personality flaw?"

Landon shrugged. "Maybe. I guess you'll just have to keep an eye on me."

"Somehow I think I'm up to the challenge," I said.

"Somehow I think you're right." Landon gave me a light kiss. "Just out of curiosity, who was your favorite princess?"

"That's a weird question."

"Don't all girls have a favorite princess?"

"I never really identified with the princesses," I said.

"You didn't like fairy tales?"

"I guess I did," I said. "I just never pictured myself wearing a crown and a fancy dress."

"Maybe that's why you stayed in your regular clothes," Landon mused.

"I don't think that's the reason," I said. "I just don't think the dress was necessary for my story. We'll have to wait and see."

"I guess," Landon said. He shifted his gaze to the tower window. "He's there."

I watched as Clove latched onto Sam's shoulders and pulled him in through the window. Sam tumbled inside, taking Clove down to the floor and out of sight. They didn't immediately return to the window.

"What do you think they're doing?" Landon asked.

"Kissing."

"Maybe Clove is transforming," Landon suggested. "Sam finished the task."

"They're still in the tower," I said. "I don't think it's going to be that easy."

As if on cue, Sam and Clove reappeared in the window. "Now what?" Sam asked.

That was a very good question. "I have no idea," I said. "Now all we've accomplished is trapping both of you in the tower."

"Sam can always climb back down," Landon said.

"I'm not leaving Clove."

Another memory niggled the back of my brain. "We can cut Clove's hair off," I said. "Do it from up there. Use it like a rope. Tie it to something and you can both climb down."

"That's a good idea," Sam said. "I'll see if I can find something to cut her hair."

"That is a good idea," Landon said. "How did you come up with it?"

"I didn't," I said. "Aunt Tillie did ... twenty years ago."

"What?"

"Ah-ha!"

I jumped when Clove shouted. Instead of fear, though, her face resonated with rage. "You scared the bejeezus out of me." She reached out and smacked someone. I was surprised when Thistle stepped into view.

"How did you get up there?" Landon asked, surprised.

"There's a door on the back side of the tower," Thistle said. "It looks as though it was hidden on this side."

"I don't understand," Sam said. "I thought I was supposed to save Clove. She's my princess."

"Oh, crap, does this mean Thistle is my prince?" Clove looked horrified.

"No one wants that," Thistle said. "I still suggest cutting your hair before we go down the stairs. They're narrow. You'll trip. Plus, you can't drag that hair through the woods."

"Fine," Clove said. "Just don't make it uneven .. and I don't care what happens, I'm not kissing you. I'm not that kind of princess."

"Yes, because that's exactly what I wanted. I wanted you to give me a big kiss. Stop wriggling! We'll be down in a minute."

Every frog could be a prince. If you're going to go around kissing them, though, you're going to have a dirty mouth. Always carry mouthwash in your purse. Not only does it make your breath smell better, if you're really in a pinch, you can throw it in someone's eyes and burn them if they get mouthy.

– *Aunt Tillie's Wonderful World of Stories to Make Little Girls Shut Up*

CHAPTER 7

"What happened to her dress?" I asked, looking Clove up and down once the three of them rejoined Landon and me on the ground. "Did it poof like yours did?"

Thistle nodded. "The second I cut her hair the dress started dissolving."

"And what happened to Sam's short shorts? I kind of miss them."

Sam scowled at me. "That's not funny."

"I wish we had our cell phones so we could've taken pictures for Facebook," Thistle said, grinning.

"Sam's outfit disappeared once he climbed through the window," Clove said. "Everything went all sparkly and the next thing I knew he was in his normal clothes."

"I wonder why," Thistle mused.

"Because he fulfilled his fairy tale," Landon said.

"How?"

"He was brave and true, just like the cricket told him to be," Landon said. "He climbed up the tower without regard for his own safety. He cared only about getting to Clove."

"And you were going to steal my princess," Sam grumbled.

Landon shot him a look. "Don't go there."

"What is he talking about?" Clove asked

"Landon was going to climb up the tower for you because he thought he was stronger," Sam said. "He stopped only because Bay was jealous."

"I was not jealous."

Thistle pressed her lips together.

"I was not jealous," I said.

Landon rubbed my shoulder to soothe me. "Listen, we have to talk about a few things before we go anywhere else," he said. "We figured out something while you guys were getting Clove out of the tower."

"Did you figure out that I'm as manly as you?" Sam asked.

"Not even remotely," Landon said, smirking.

"We figured out that the curse is keying in on certain ... personality traits," I said. "Our personality faults, if you want to be more precise."

"Oh, crap," Thistle said. "That's why we're arguing nonstop."

"You've been arguing nonstop?" Clove's eyes widened. "That's horrible."

"This is bad," Thistle said. "This means Clove is going to be even more of a Pollyanna than usual, Bay is going to be more insecure than usual, Landon is going to be more bossy than usual and Sam is going to be ... huh ... what's your biggest personality flaw?"

"I don't have one," Sam said.

"He's got the ego thing with Landon," I said.

"Hey," Landon said. "I thought we decided to call it a hero complex?"

"Sorry, honey," I said, smiling at him before rolling my eyes in Thistle's direction. "This also means that you're going to be more ... bitchy ... than usual. Can you say that word in a fairy tale land? Probably not. You're going to be more whiny than usual."

"I am not whiny," Thistle said.

"You're totally whiny," Clove said, laughing. "I'm not a Pollyanna, though."

"You're a total Pollyanna," Thistle said.

"Don't listen to her, sweetheart," Sam said, slipping his arm around

Clove's waist and pulling her close. "She's trying to get under your skin the way she always does."

"Which means that's going to be amplified while we're here," I said. "We all have to make a concerted effort to control ourselves. Think before you speak."

"Does that go for you, too?" Thistle challenged.

"Yes," I said. "I'm the one who had the huge bout of jealousy when Landon wanted to climb up after Clove. I'm also the one who had the big jolt of insecurity when I woke up in the bear cabin alone."

"You didn't tell me about that," Thistle said. "What did you think? Did you think Landon got up in the middle of the night and abandoned you?"

My cheeks burned under Thistle's studied gaze. "I ... ."

"Oh, this really is a cluster of crap," Thistle said. "Everything we hate about ourselves is going to keep popping up. You hate that you still worry about Landon walking out again, so that's exactly the first conclusion you jumped to when you woke up alone. Clove has a persecution complex, and she's going to spend the next ... however long we're stuck here ... thinking we're talking behind her back. This is officially a nightmare."

"What do you hate about yourself?" Landon asked.

"We're not going to talk about that," Thistle said. "We need to figure a way out of this before we all implode, though. If we're not careful, we're going to do a lot worse than we usually do when we start arguing."

"Speaking of nightmares, are we sure this isn't a dream?" Clove asked. "Just because we've never messed with dream magic before, that doesn't mean Aunt Tillie wouldn't risk doing it now."

"She might," I conceded. "That was one of the few rules she really drilled into us, though. I think it's something else."

"What?"

"I've been giving that some thought," I said, pushing my hair from my forehead and exhaling heavily. "I remembered something when Clove was in the tower. That's how I knew her hair had to be cut off."

"What did you remember?"

"*Aunt Tillie's Wonderful World of Stories to Make Little Girls Shut Up.*"

"What?" Landon sputtered, chuckling heartily.

"What is that?" Sam asked.

"Oh, no," Thistle said. "You're right. Oh, son of a … . That's exactly what this is."

"I think I'm missing something," Clove said. "What are you guys talking about?"

"It's the book she used to read to us when our mothers put her in charge of our bedtime stories," I reminded her. "Mom always told her to read fairy tales and children's books to us after she caught her reading that V.C. Andrews book in our bedroom one night and almost had an aneurysm."

"That was the incest book, right?"

"That you remember," Thistle muttered. "You don't remember *Aunt Tillie's Wonderful World of Stories to Make Little Girls Shut Up*, but you remember the really creepy attic sex between a brother and a sister. Nice."

"The only reason I remember it is because they had those movies on Lifetime a few months ago," Clove replied, defensively. "I'm not some creepy pervert." She glanced at Sam for support. "I'm not."

"I don't care how perverted you are," Sam said. "Tell me more about this book Aunt Tillie read to you guys."

"Once she was caught reading that book our mothers made her promise she would read us only fairy tales before bed," I said. "The problem is, Aunt Tillie doesn't like fairy tales. She thinks they're stupid."

"They are stupid," Landon said.

"They've survived and thrived for a reason," I said. "Most of them have little lessons wrapped in pretty stories about fairies and princesses and talking bears. Aunt Tillie never liked them, though."

"She took the traditional stories and altered them," Thistle said. "She even created a book so she would have something to read when she was stuck with bedtime duty. I'll bet you she cursed us into that book. We're not asleep. We're in the book."

"Altered them how?"

"She put her own spin on them," I said.

Clove clapped her hand to her mouth. "Oh. I'm remembering them. The Rapunzel one had something to do with cutting your own hair off instead of waiting around for a prince to save you. She said only someone truly pathetic would spend years in a tower when she could get herself out."

"Exactly," I said. "The moral of the three bears in the house wasn't that they offered comfort to a stranger. It was that you were supposed to remember not to touch other people's property. If I had stayed in the cabin any longer, the bears would have tried to eat me if I touched any of their stuff in front of them. I got lucky. I was too afraid to touch anything."

"What about the mermaid?" Landon asked.

"Aunt Tillie was convinced that anyone who swam around with a seashell bra had to be loose," Thistle said. "I think that one was pretty self-explanatory."

"What about the turtle?" Landon pressed.

"I don't remember that one," Thistle said.

"It obviously had something to do with having faith," I said. "I can't remember that one either."

"What other stories are we looking at here?" Sam asked, worried.

"She made up a new one every night," I said. "I can't remember all of them, but I know some were all takes on the classics, while others were figments of her imagination."

"I remember Snow White, Cinderella and Sleeping Beauty – but mostly because those were my favorite stories," Clove said.

"You always did like the ones where the heroine danced and sang," I said. "I forgot that about you."

"I remember the Wonderland one," Thistle said. "I always loved that story and Aunt Tillie completely ruined it for me. All that talk of creepy tea parties and talking rabbits. I'm still terrified of that bunny they trot out at the mall every Easter to take photos with the kids."

"What was the point of the Pinocchio one?" Sam asked. "Why was the dude in the store so creepy?"

"Aunt Tillie said anyone who spent all his time whittling wood and dreaming about little boys wasn't really father material," Clove said. "I remember that one. I've been afraid of puppets ever since."

"You're not the only one," I said. "Puppets freak me out."

"They're better than clowns," Landon muttered.

"It's okay, sweetie," I said, running my finger down the side of his face. "I'll keep the clowns away from you. I promise."

"He's afraid of clowns? That's rich," Thistle said, snickering. "Is it because of the clown in *It*? It's always because of Pennywise."

"Leave him alone," I said. "He's had a rough night."

"We've all had a rough night," Clove said. "The question is: What do we do now? How do we get ourselves out of the book?"

"We have to find Marcus first," Thistle said. "If we're all here, he has to be here, too. You promised we would find him next."

"We are," Landon said. "We have to figure out where he is."

"Well, let's think about this," Thistle said, rubbing the back of her neck. "We've all been in relatively close proximity to each other. I don't think he can be very far away.

Ribbit.

Thistle stilled. "No way."

"What?" Clove asked.

Ribbit.

"This can't be happening," Thistle said, swiveling quickly. "That frog is back. I swear, I'm going to kill it."

"Why did it follow us?" Landon asked. "We've come a long way from that pond. It couldn't have been easy for it to follow across such a big distance."

"I don't care," Thistle said. "I'm going to squash it. I can't stand that sound. It's going to drive me crazy."

Thistle was short-tempered on a normal day. This was definitely not a normal day.

The frog croaked so loudly it almost sounded like screaming. That's when I realized what was going on. "Don't!"

Thistle froze, her eyes dark and her foot raised. "Why?"

"I think it's Marcus," I said.

"Marcus? You think Marcus is a frog? That's ridiculous." Thistle was doubtful, but still she lowered her foot.

"Is it?" I asked. "Isn't the *The Frog Prince* a fairy tale?"

"It is," Clove said. She pushed past Thistle and leaned down, staring the frog in the eye. "Are you Marcus?"

Ribbit.

"Oh, I think Bay is right. I think this is Marcus."

Thistle was livid. She reached over and scooped up the frog, lifting it so she could stare into its tiny eyes. "Marcus? Can this really be him?"

"Why else would the frog follow us from the pond?" I asked. "Landon woke up in a different fairy tale, but he was still close to me. We ran into each other first. I think we accidentally skipped over Marcus. That's when we found Sam, and Clove wasn't far from him. I think this is Marcus."

"How do we change him back?" Thistle asked, mortified.

"Um ... well ... ." I glanced at Clove for support, but her smile was both evil and gleeful.

"You have to kiss it," Clove said. "That's what happens in the fairy tale."

"I am not kissing a frog. I'm just not going to do it. We don't even know that this is Marcus."

"Does anyone remember what Aunt Tillie said in her version of that fairy tale?" Landon asked.

"Just that if you were going to go around kissing frogs and trying to turn them into princes you should wash your mouth out when you're done," I replied.

Landon chortled. "Oh, this is priceless. I don't even know what to say. I feel as if I'm going crazy."

"You're not the one expected to kiss a frog," Thistle said.

"Just do it," Landon said. "We have to know."

Thistle stared at the frog a second and then she shoved it in my face. "You kiss it."

"I'm not kissing that frog," I said, pushing her hand back. "Besides, I already have my prince. You have to kiss it. He's your ... frog prince."

"This is ludicrous," Thistle said, pulling the frog back and lifting it closer to her face. "I'm going to do this, but only because I'll never forgive myself if this really is Marcus and I let him stay in this state for one second longer than I have to."

"Good," I said. "Pucker up!"

"I hate you for this," Thistle said. "This is all your fault."

"How do you figure that?"

"I haven't decided yet, but the second I can find a way to blame it on you I will," Thistle said.

"I'll be waiting."

"Oh, and you're officially dead to me."

"I'm used to that," I said.

"Okay," Thistle said, inhaling a steadying breath. "This isn't going to be so bad. It's just a frog. It's not like it's a snake … or a rat … or a clown."

"I'm never going to live this clown stuff down, am I?" Landon complained.

"Probably not," I said, slipping my hand into his.

Thistle pressed her lips together, resigned, and then leaned forward. "Oh, crap. Here we go." The second her lips touched the frog a bright green light flared and the frog disappeared from her hand.

I shielded my eyes from the blinding light, and when I dared turn back I wasn't surprised to see Marcus standing in front of Thistle.

Thistle pulled back, her eyes wide. "It was you!"

"It's about time," Marcus grumbled. "Do you have any idea how hard it was to follow you guys as a freaking frog?"

Thistle's face went from happy to sad within an instant, and then she promptly burst into tears. "I'm so sorry. You'll never know how sorry I am."

Marcus was taken aback. "I … it's okay." He rubbed Thistle's back worriedly and pulled her in for a hug. "It's not as if you knew."

"I was going to stomp on you," Thistle sobbed, tears running down her face.

"We wouldn't have let you stomp on him," I said.

"I almost stepped on you," Thistle said. "I'm a horrible person."

"You're not a horrible person," Marcus said, kissing her cheek. "You didn't know. It's okay. We're all together now. Everything is going to be okay."

Marcus held her close and then began to sway, rocking her as she cried.

"It's okay," he whispered over and over.

"Well, we're all together," Landon said. "Now what?"

"I'm ready to wake up," Sam said.

"I think we're all ready for that," Landon said. "How do we make that happen? How do we get out of the book?"

If seven strangers offer to help you, run the other way. Men don't run around together unless they're in gangs. Well, sometimes they run around together if they're trying to sell you a pack of lies, too – or a nice bridge.

– Aunt Tillie's Wonderful World of Stories to Make Little Girls Shut Up

CHAPTER 8

"I don't think we can magically get out of the book," I said. Thistle had stopped crying, although she didn't look particularly happy. Marcus kept her wrapped tight against him, her face pressed to his chest, and he was still swaying. "We have to finish the story," Thistle said. "That's what you think, isn't it?"

I nodded. "Aunt Tillie isn't the type of person to let us walk away because we finished a few fairy tales. She promised retribution, and she needs us tied up for a long time. We're going to have to finish the book."

"She warned us that she was going to do something," Clove said. "We should have expected it."

"How were we supposed to foresee her cursing us into a book?" I asked.

"I don't know," Clove said. "I feel like we missed some obvious signs."

"We can't focus on that right now," Landon said. "We have to start working our way through this world, and we need to do it faster than we have been doing it."

"What if our mothers are here?" Clove asked.

"I don't think they are," I said. "I'm sure she did something else to them. This was for us specifically. We're uniquely qualified to solve this because she created it for us."

"I feel so loved," Thistle growled. "It's not every great-aunt who creates a horrible fairy tale world to curse her nieces. It's like I'm the luckiest girl in the world."

"As much as I'm loving the pity party, we need to move on from this place," Landon said. "We're obviously done here. We can keep talking. Let's just do it while we're walking."

"Yes, sir," Thistle said, mock saluting.

While I didn't think the sass was necessary – or helpful – I was glad to see the color returning to her cheeks and the snarkiness taking up residence in her voice again.

Landon narrowed his eyes but wisely bit his tongue. After an ugly staredown, he turned his attention to me. "Which way now, sweetie?"

"Why are you asking her?" Clove asked.

"She hasn't led us astray yet," Landon said. "She knew how to find Thistle and she led us to Sam. I say we stick with her intuition."

"I don't think it's going to matter," Thistle said. "I think we could pick any direction and we'd still stumble upon the next chapter in the story."

"I still want Bay to choose," Landon said. "Is that too much to ask?"

"Whatever," Thistle said. "Come on, Princess Bay. Pick a direction."

I ignored the sarcasm and pressed my eyes shut, feeling a tug to the right. "There," I said, pointing.

Landon grabbed my hand and started pulling me. "Let's go."

"He's really alpha right now," Marcus said.

"That's because the curse is also making us give in to all of our personality defects," Thistle explained. "Bay is insecure. Landon is bossy. Sam is defensive. Clove is a Pollyanna."

"What are you?" Marcus asked.

"Relieved to have found you."

Marcus smiled and gave her a soft kiss. "That's very cute. I don't believe you, though. I'm guessing you're complaining a lot more than usual, which is a frightening thought."

"I hate this night," Thistle grumbled.

"It's okay," Marcus said. "We're together now. I'll take care of you. I'm your prince, right?"

"That's kind of insulting."

"You'll live."

"How do we know where we're going?" Clove asked.

"I just had a feeling to come this way," I said, pushing through some overhanging tree branches. "I don't know why."

I sucked in a breath when I reached the other side of the trees. This couldn't be good.

"I have a feeling I know why you picked this way to come," Landon said, his eyes landing on the yellow sidewalk cutting a winding path through the woods.

"Is that what I think it is?" Thistle asked.

"It's a yellow brick road."

"That's not a fairy tale, though," Sam said. "It was a movie."

"It was based on a book, and it's technically considered to be the first American fairy tale," Clove said.

"How do you know that?"

"It's my favorite book."

"Oh," Sam said. "That means this is probably going to be a fairy tale for you, doesn't it?"

"We won't know until we find out where the path leads," I said. "Let's get moving."

"I'm warning you guys right now, if there are flying monkeys I'm out of here," Marcus said.

"You're afraid of flying monkeys?" an obviously tickled Thistle asked.

"They gave me nightmares when I was a kid," Marcus conceded.

"Well, we can put your monkeys in a room with Landon's clowns and have a free-for-all," Thistle laughed.

"Way to get a handle on that bitchy thing, Thistle," Landon said.

"Way to get a handle on that bossy thing, Landon," Thistle shot back.

"Everyone shut up," I said. "Can we have five minutes of silence? Please?"

Landon and Thistle made twin faces of disgust.

"I agree with Bay," Marcus said. "This is getting out of hand."

"Maybe you should be Bay's prince, then," Thistle said. "You obviously like her temperament better than mine."

"Don't even joke about that," Landon said. "I'm hanging on to my princess and Marcus is definitely hanging on to his. I don't want his princess. Good grief … the things I'm saying tonight are just flabbergasting."

"Can we please walk down the yellow road for five minutes without sniping at each other?" I asked. "Just five minutes?"

"Fine," Thistle conceded. "After that, though, I'm going nuts."

"That's going to be a short trip," Landon said.

"HAS it been five minutes yet?"

"I'm going to have to kill her," Landon muttered under his breath.

I gripped his hand tighter. "I know this is hard for you. I'm sorry."

Landon's face softened. "You don't have anything to be sorry about," he said. "You didn't do this."

"My family did, though."

"Bay, I love you," Landon said. "I'm not angry with you. I'm angry at this situation. I'm sorry I'm being so … obnoxious. I can't seem to help myself."

"None of us can."

"I just … oh, someone tell me what that is."

We slowed our pace and focused on the small figures standing in the middle of the road about twenty feet in front of us. I had no idea where they came from, but they were here now.

"I'm guessing we're about to embark on Snow White," I said.

"What makes you say that?"

"There are little people standing over there," I said.

"Maybe they're munchkins. We are on the yellow brick road, after all."

"No, they're dwarves," Thistle said. "Look. They're holding axes … and there are seven of them."

"Is anyone else worried that they're holding axes?" Sam asked.

"I'm not thrilled with it," Landon said. "Everyone be ready to run if it becomes necessary. Just … be careful."

We slowly approached the dwarves, and I pasted a bright smile on my face as we drew close. "Hi. Who are you guys?"

"Way to not make this awkward, sweetie," Landon said. "Just forego all those little conversational pleasantries that make people more comfortable around strangers."

"I thought you were in a hurry?"

"I still don't want to tick the little guys with the axes off," Landon said. "Now … get behind me."

I rolled my eyes.

"We're not little guys," the first dwarf said. "We're dwarves."

"We figured that out," Thistle said.

"What gave it away?"

"The axes."

"That usually does it," the dwarf said. "I guess I should introduce us."

"That would be great," I said.

"I'm … ."

"Wait, let me guess," Thistle said. "You're Grumpy."

"Well, it hasn't been a great day, but I'm not grumpy."

"I thought that was your name," Thistle said, disappointed.

"No, my name is Flip."

"Flip?"

"Flip."

"Huh," Thistle said. "I don't remember this part of the story."

Flip ignored her. "This is Kip, Trip, Skip, Pip, Whip and Bud."

Well, that sounded fun.

"Bud?" Thistle asked. "Your mother couldn't think of one more name that ended with 'ip?'"

"Apparently not," Flip said. "It's been a lifelong embarrassment for Bud. He doesn't talk much."

I studied Bud for a moment. "He doesn't look happy with his lot in life."

"Would you be happy with our lot in life?" Flip asked. "We spend twelve hours a day digging in mines and we don't even get paid for it."

"So stop doing it," Thistle said.

"We can't," Flip said. "We're dwarves. That's what we do."

The rest of his brothers nodded in enthusiastic agreement.

Landon cleared his throat. "So, um, is there a reason you're hanging around the yellow brick road?"

"We're waiting for someone," Flip said.

"Who?"

"Snow White."

"I told you," I crowed.

"You're the smartest woman in the world, sweetie," Landon said, refusing to let me slide out of the arm cage he'd built behind him to corral me.

"Do you know what Snow White looks like?" Sam asked.

Flip nodded.

"Do you know when she's supposed to get here?"

"She's already here," Flip said.

"Oh, this is going to be bad," Thistle said. "Does anyone remember whether the dwarves gang-banged Snow White in Aunt Tillie's story? I'm really worried about that for some reason."

"We're not sexual deviants," Flip said. "We just need her to clean our cabin and sing while we're at work."

"Sing?"

"Sing."

"Which one of us do you think is Snow White?" a nervous Clove asked.

Since she was the only one with dark hair, we all expected it to be her.

Flip grinned at her. "Welcome home."

"Oh, no way," Clove shouted. "I just spent two hours in a tower waiting for someone to climb my hair. I'm absolutely not turning myself into a maid and … singing."

"You have to," Flip said. "That's what you do."

"Well, I'm not going to do it," Clove said. "I'm drawing the line. I'm done. This fairy tale world sucks."

"It does suck," Landon said.

"Listen, I have no idea who the rest of you are, but we need to claim our Snow White before it gets too late," Flip said.

"Yeah, we want dinner," Trip said. "We haven't had a decent meal in ten years."

"How did you know to wait here for Snow White?" I asked.

"The crone told us."

"What crone?"

"The one in the black dress and hood with the red apple," Flip said. "She said Snow White was coming and we were to wait here until she crossed our path. We've been here a long time."

"How long?"

"A couple of hours."

I rubbed the back of my neck, weary. "Does anyone have any suggestions?" I asked. "It's not as if we can let Clove go with the dwarves. If that story plays out, she's going to eat a poison apple and then land in a glass coffin."

"Yeah, I'd really rather not die," Clove said.

"We need to move this along," Landon said. "Um, guys, here's the thing ... you can't have Snow White. I don't know what this crone told you, and I'm really curious what she looks like because I'm picturing a tiny woman with a round face and evil eyes ... ."

"How did you know that?" Flip asked.

"Just a lucky guess," Landon said, grimacing.

He'd described Aunt Tillie. Had she really based some of the characters in the book on herself? That made sense. She always thought she was the center of all of our worlds.

"The thing is, the crone's information is outdated," Landon said, and I could practically see his mind working. "It seems Snow White can't do any manual labor until her contract is settled."

"What contract?"

"Yeah, what contract?" Clove asked.

Landon shot her a quelling look. "Snow White joined a union."

"No way," Flip said. "Is that even allowed?"

"It's a new world, man," Landon said. "She's on strike until the contract is settled."

"When is that going to happen?" Flip asked. "We really need a maid."

"I suggest hiring the crone," I said. "She's great with a broom ... and a cackle."

"And she sings like a dream," Thistle said. "This one over here is tone deaf."

"I am not," Clove protested. "I have a beautiful singing voice."

"Since when?" Thistle asked, laughing. "You're so off key you scare small children and household pets."

"That's not true," Clove said. "Bay, tell her that's not true."

I worried my bottom lip with my teeth, unsure how to progress. The truth was, Clove wasn't a terrible singer. She was awful. Thistle wasn't exaggerating. There's nothing worse than someone who thinks they can sing when they really can't. Usually I go out of my way to spare Clove's feelings – especially at times like this – but we needed the dwarves to give up their maid quest.

"When you sing you sound like the frog Thistle had to kiss," I said.

Clove crossed her arms over her chest, jutting out her lower lip. "You're dead to me."

We were all going to be dead to each other if we didn't get out of this book. "You'll live."

"I'm not sure I believe you guys," Flip said. "Can we hear this alleged bad singing?"

"Sure," I said.

Clove balked. "But ... I need time to warm up. I need a piano to accompany me. I need ... my karaoke machine."

"We don't have any of that," I said.

"And we're in a bit of a time crunch here," Landon added. "Just sing, scare them and get it over with. I don't want to spend any more time here than we have to."

"I'm not going to scare them," Clove said. "If I sing, they're all going to fall in love with me. Isn't that right, Sam?"

Sam looked trapped. "I happen to find your singing ... cute," he said. "I especially like when you do it in the shower."

Thistle snorted. "I'm guessing that's because you're naked, Clove."

"Shut up," Clove said. "You're dead to me, too."

"Just sing," I said. "Pick a song and ... wow them. Prove us all wrong. You know that's what you want to do."

"What are you doing?" Landon murmured. "What happens if she can really sing?"

"She can't."

"What if the curse made it so she can sing?"

I hadn't thought of that. Uh-oh. I opened my mouth to stop Clove from belting out a Broadway tune – I just knew we had a rendition of *Memory* in our future – but it was too late.

Clove began to sing, her eyes wide and her chest puffed out. It was her proudest moment. And then the birds started complaining ... loudly. A couple of them even swooped down in an attack formation.

The deer in the field next to the dwarves bounded away. The rabbits in the nearby bush tried to burrow beneath it to drown her out.

Then the dwarves started groaning and covering their ears.

Clove broke off, flummoxed. "What's wrong?"

Flip arched an eyebrow. "We believe you," he said. "Keep her on strike. I'd rather live in filth than live with ... that."

"What are you talking about?" Clove was incensed. "I could be on *American Idol*."

"You could," Thistle said, patting her shoulder. "You could be on those first few episodes where they let the really bad singers in so they can laugh at them."

"I really hate you," Clove said.

When we glanced back up the yellow brick road, the dwarves were gone. They'd opted to beat a hasty retreat while we were distracted. It was probably for the best.

Landon released his grip on me, finally allowing a small smile to play at the corner of his lips. "This is just so ... messed up."

"Aren't you glad I don't sing? I sound worse than her."

"Sweetie, if we get out of this, I'll listen to you sing every day for the rest of my life," Landon said.

That was kind of sweet.

"I'll just put headphones on and watch you dance naked or something."

His sweetness comes and goes.

"Let's get moving," Landon said. "I have a feeling we have a few more fairy tales to go through before we can say 'the end.'"

I had a feeling he was right.

If you're going to cry wolf, you'd better hope there's really a wolf there. Oh, and if there's a wolf, kick it really hard in its special place before you run. Wolves are faster than little girls.

– *Aunt Tillie's Wonderful World of Stories to Make Little Girls Shut Up*

CHAPTER 9

"I don't care what anyone says," Clove said. "I can sing. The curse must have made me sound horrible or something."

"I'm sure that was it," Sam said, rubbing her back lightly as he directed her down the pathway. "You sound like an angel when you sing."

"It's probably good you're not Pinocchio right now," Thistle said. "Your nose would be about five feet long if you were."

"Shut up, Thistle," Sam grumbled. "Why do you always have to be so ... you?"

Thistle frowned, her forehead furrowing. "I'm sorry. You're right."

Everyone shifted their attention to her, surprised.

"Oh, don't do that," Thistle said. "I'm well aware of how annoying I can be. I'm really trying not to say everything that crosses my mind, but it's not easy."

"It's not easy for any of us," Landon said. "We have to keep moving forward. We don't have a lot of options here. We have to get to the end of the book, and to do that we can't kill each other."

"Speaking of that, do you think we die in the real world if we die in this story?" Marcus asked.

I'd been wondering that myself. "I don't know," I said. "I'd like to think Aunt Tillie wouldn't risk our lives unnecessarily, but she was really ticked off last night."

"She wouldn't risk our lives," Clove said. "I know she wouldn't."

"What if she didn't realize she did?" Thistle asked. "We don't know where her mind was when she cast the curse. I mean, this has all the elements of being well thought out, but she had to cast it on the fly."

"Maybe it's something she had in her back pocket for a long time," I suggested. "Maybe she came up with the idea years ago, but decided she can finally utilize it. That sounds like something she would do."

"It does," Thistle conceded. "The amount of thought she put into this, though … it's just amazing."

"I always thought she liked me," Marcus said. "I never thought I would make it onto her list."

"If it's any consolation, I don't think you made it on her list," I said. "I think Landon was on her list, and I think she knew she was going to have to distract Thistle, Clove and me, but I think you and Sam were included because she needed an even number of princesses and princes."

"That was one of her complaints about fairy tales," Thistle said. "She didn't understand why princesses were considered heroines when their only goal seemed to be snagging a man."

Landon barked out a hoarse laugh. "I guess I never thought about it that way. There are fairy tales that don't involve coupling up, though."

"I think Aunt Tillie just wanted us to shut up when we were kids," Thistle said. "Clove went through a princess phase, but Bay and I never did. Bay went through a stuffed animal phase and I preferred Legos. It's not as if we were walking around dreaming about princes."

"And yet you got them," Marcus teased, poking her in the ribs.

"We did," Thistle said, tilting her head to the side and rubbing her forehead.

"Do you have a headache?" Marcus asked, worried.

"I'm just exhausted," Thistle said. "We only got a couple of hours of sleep before the curse hit, and it feels like we've been at this for hours. How long do you think it's been?"

I shrugged. I had no idea.

"I'm guessing between four and five hours," Landon said. "Without any changes in the sky, though, it's really hard to tell. I never realized how much I used the sun to gauge the time of day."

"I use the clock on my cell phone," Clove said.

"I think the lack of sun is throwing off our internal clocks," Landon said.

"I don't think that's the only thing," Thistle said. "I feel as if I have PMS."

Marcus, Sam and Landon made identical horrified faces.

"That's not supposed to happen for two weeks," Landon said. "I marked it on my calendar."

"That's disturbing," I said.

"You three are disturbing when you're feeling moody together," Landon said. "If I can keep you away from those two you're fine. Well, you're not fine, but you're tolerable. If you three get together, though? Good night. It's like the end of the world."

"Bring me ice cream," Sam said, mimicking Clove's voice to perfection.

"My back hurts," Marcus said.

"My pants are too tight," Landon said.

I narrowed my eyes and put my hands on my hips. "Is that how I sound to you?"

Landon grinned. "Sometimes."

"Well, you don't have to worry about me ever talking to you again then," I muttered.

"And here we go with the mood swings," Landon said. "This night keeps getting worse. Every time I think it's not possible … ."

Thistle scowled. "I didn't mean that it's that time of the month," she said. "I mean that I can't seem to control my emotions. One second I'm fine. I wouldn't say I'm comfortable or happy, but I'm not panicking or anything. The next second it's as if every bad impulse I've ever had just … takes over."

"I know the feeling," I said. "I felt like crying for absolutely no reason a few minutes ago."

"What were you thinking about?" Clove asked. "I was going to cry a few minutes ago, too, but I know why I was going to do it."

"Because we made fun of your singing," Thistle said.

"Exactly."

"I don't know," I said. "I don't want to sit here and dissect everything. I'm so tired. I just want to be back in my bed. I want to rub my feet against Landon's and listen to him sleep. That sounds like the best thing in the world right now."

Landon arched an eyebrow. "You listen to me sleep?"

"Don't let it inflate your ego," I said. "Sometimes when I wake up in the middle of the night it's the sound of your breathing that lulls me right back to sleep. I can't explain it."

"I do the same thing, sweetie," Landon said, tightening his grip on my hand. "I would seriously buy Aunt Tillie a new snowplow if we could only get out of this book."

"I don't think it's going to be that easy," I said. "We have to keep walking."

"We should sing a song to make the trip go faster," Clove suggested. "I can start."

"No!"

"**HELP!**"

"Did you hear that?" Landon asked.

Twenty minutes later we were still walking down the path in morose silence. Clove was pouting about the singing. I was pouting about my deep thoughts. And Thistle, well, she was pouting because she felt like it. I think the men were happy for the conversational reprieve.

"Did someone scream for help? Yeah, it was hard to miss," Thistle replied dryly.

"Help!"

Landon glanced at me. "Are we going to ignore that?"

I worried my bottom lip, unsure. "I think we have to find our way to the end of the path. This is probably just a way to delay us."

"Help! Please!"

Landon pressed his eyes shut, trying to block out the voice.

"Help!"

"I can't ignore that," he said. "I ... I'm supposed to help people."

I let go of his hand. This was clearly his fairy tale puzzle to solve. "Go."

Landon bolted off the path and into the night, racing down a hill and disappearing into a grove of trees.

"Should we follow him?" Thistle asked.

"Yeah. I don't want to risk being separated."

"He's going to wish he'd stayed on the path," Clove said. "He's going to be angry with himself."

"I know," I said. "He can't listen to someone ask for help and not offer it, though. It's not in him. Let's go."

We followed Landon down the embankment and through the trees. The cries for help ceased, but somehow I knew which direction to go. I found Landon standing in the middle of a field, a herd of sheep happily munching grass around him, and fixed him with a quizzical look. "Who was screaming?"

Landon shifted so I could see the young boy standing next to him. The boy was small, his skin pale, his gangly limbs gesturing emphatically as he pointed at the field.

"Who are you?" I asked.

"Daniel," the boy said, flashing me an impish grin.

"What are you doing out here, Daniel?" I asked, forcing my face to reflect welcome even though my stomach was churning. Landon may need to save people, but I sensed right away that something else was going on here.

"I'm watching the sheep," Daniel said.

"Do they do tricks?" Thistle asked.

"No way," Daniel said. "They just munch and dump."

"That's a nice visual," Thistle said, causing me to crack a real smile. She clearly didn't trust him either.

"Should you be out here alone at night?" Landon asked, his cop face in place. "Where are your parents?"

"They're at home," Daniel replied. "Watching the sheep is my job."

"You're awfully young to have a job," Landon said.

"Um, Landon, this isn't the real world," Thistle reminded him. "No one is running afoul of child labor laws."

Landon ignored her. "Don't you think it's dangerous to be out here?"

"Not really," Daniel said, unruffled. "The only thing dangerous out here is the wolf."

"Wolf?"

Oh, crap. I had a feeling I knew which story we were in. It was the one Aunt Tillie always warned us about as children when we started screaming and tattling on one another. "Landon … ."

"It's huge," Daniel said, his eyes sparkling. "It's like eight feet tall, and it walks on its hind legs and it steals sheep if I don't watch out for it."

"And your parents think it's safe for you to be out here watching the sheep even though there's a wolf on the prowl?" Landon didn't look convinced.

"We make our money off the sheep," Daniel explained. "They have to be watched. That's my job."

"I think I should talk to your parents," Landon said.

"That's not part of the story," I said. "His parents have nothing to do with this … tale."

"And what tale is that?" Landon asked, shifting his eyes to me.

"He's the boy who cried wolf."

Landon furrowed his brow, confused. "You're saying he's making it up?"

"It's one of Aunt Tillie's favorite stories," Thistle said. "She always accused us of doing it when we were kids."

I hated the conflicted look on Landon's face. He believed us, and yet the idea of leaving a child out in a field to fend for himself didn't sit right with him. "How can you be sure the wolf isn't real? There are wolves in fairy tales all of the time."

"There are," I conceded. "Even if it is real, though, this is still just a story. This isn't real."

"I'm real," Daniel said. "I'm right here."

I smiled at him kindly. "I know. I think you should probably call it a night, though, and go back home. That would be best for everyone."

"What about the sheep?"

"I'm sure they'll still be here in the morning," I said. Hopefully we wouldn't be here to make sure.

"I can't," Daniel said. "It's my job to watch the sheep."

"I still want to talk to your parents," Landon said. "Where are they?"

"I already told you," Daniel said. "They're home."

"Landon, we don't have time to walk miles to this kid's house and have a deep discussion about parental obligations with them," I said. "That's not why we're here."

"Isn't this my tale?"

I nodded.

"Then I'm going to talk to his parents."

I wanted to shake him back to his senses. Instead, I turned to Marcus for support. If Landon was going to listen to anyone it would be him. "Marcus, what do you think we should do?"

The grim set of Marcus' jaw told me he wasn't thrilled with the question. "I don't like the idea of the kid being out here alone either."

I shook my head, frustrated. "But ... ."

Marcus cut me off. "But we're not here for this. It's another distraction," he said. "We need to go back to the road and keep going. We're wasting time here."

Landon tightened his grip on Daniel's shoulder. "I know you're right. It's just ... it feels wrong."

I understood why Landon was the one drawn into this tale. It was something I often worried about where he was concerned. He cared more than any person should – or feasibly could – when it came to the safety of others. He was overcome by the need to save everyone.

I reached out to him tentatively. Instead of pulling away as I feared he would, though, he grabbed my hand and took a step away from Daniel. "Try to stay safe," Landon said.

Daniel rolled his eyes. "I'm always safe."

"Watch the sheep," Thistle said. "That's your job, and you need to do your job."

"I know," Daniel said.

Landon let me lead him away, and we were almost through the trees when his belief in me came crashing down.

"Wolf! Help! Wolf! It's going to eat me!"

Landon jerked his hand from mine and turned, running back in the direction of Daniel's screams. I didn't hesitate to follow him, and when we returned to the field Daniel was standing right where we left him. He was alone, other than the munching and dumping sheep, of course.

"Where's the wolf?" Landon asked, scanning the field.

"I saw him for only a second. "He had glowing red eyes and fangs that were this big," said Daniel, spreading his arms wide for emphasis. "He was going to eat me."

Landon exhaled heavily before turning back to face me. "You were right."

"It's not about being right," I said. "This is the world Aunt Tillie created. We could leave this field a hundred times. Each one of those times he's going to try to stop us by screaming and carrying on about wolves. We're never going to see a wolf. Not in this tale."

"I'm sorry," Landon said. "I should have left."

"You're not the type of person who abandons someone," I said. "Even when you didn't know me, you never abandoned me. I seem to keep forgetting that. You got shot for me, and you had no idea what kind of person I was.

"I know you want to save everyone," I said. "That's not what's happening here, though."

"I know," Landon said, weary. "Let's get moving. I'm sure there are other horrors waiting around the next bend."

"That's something to look forward to," I teased.

"It is," Landon agreed, grabbing my hand.

We were almost back to the trees when Daniel decided to speak again. "Wait ... you're not going to leave me here with the wolf, are you?"

"I guess so," Landon replied, refusing to turn around. "Try to stay safe, kid."

"But ... ."

Daniel didn't finish whatever he was about to say. Instead, he let loose with a blood-curdling scream. Even though I knew it was a game, I couldn't stop myself from turning around. Instead of Daniel's mischievous smile, though, I saw his look of terror as a large monster descended on the boy.

"Holy crap!"

Landon whipped around, stunned.

The wolf paid us no heed, instead grabbing Daniel around the waist and hoisting him over his shoulder. Daniel was right. This was no normal wolf. It walked on two legs and its eyes were ... human. They were full of malevolence, although they weren't glowing and red, but they were still human.

"Help me," Daniel screamed, pounding on the wolf's back.

We couldn't do anything but stand there, though. We were frozen in place and we watched the wolf carry Daniel into the woods. Just like that ... he was gone.

If a wolf can fool you by putting on a nightcap and glasses, you've got bigger problems than the wolf. That also means you're either blind or stupid. I'd rather fight a wolf than be stupid.

– Aunt Tillie's Wonderful World of Stories to Make Little Girls Shut Up

CHAPTER 10

"What just happened here?" I was at a loss for words.

"What just happened here?" Landon repeated, turning to face off with me. "You said there was no wolf."

"I ... ."

"That looked like a wolf to me."

"Calm down," Marcus said, pushing between Landon and me. It was a useless move. Landon would never put his hands on me, but his face was so red with anger I didn't blame Marcus for being worried. "We all thought he was the boy who cried wolf."

"What are you doing?" Landon asked, looking Marcus up and down. "Do you really think I'm going to hurt her?"

"I'm worried that you seem a little ... intense," Marcus said.

Landon faltered. "I would never hurt her."

"I know, man," Marcus said, taking a step back. "I'm sorry. I don't know why I thought that."

"It's this place," Thistle said. "The longer we're here, the more it's messing with us. Aunt Tillie knew what she was doing when she cast the curse."

"It's not only the worst parts of ourselves that are coming out now," I said, wrapping my hand around Landon's wrist briefly. When I moved to pull it away he placed his other hand over it and held it there. "We're taking on characteristics of the story characters themselves now."

"When did you figure that out?" Clove asked.

"I don't know," I said. "I've been thinking about it for a little while, I guess. It's the reason I feel as if I'm going to start crying. Aunt Tillie always said the women in most fairy tales were weak.

"I think it's also the reason Thistle is getting ... grumpier ... as we go on," I continued. "She's turning into a ... villain."

"Is that what's happening to me?" Landon asked, worried.

"I don't know," I said. "The men in the stories are ... different. There's more room for conflict. I mean, think about it. Snow White, Cinderella, Rapunzel ... all of them ... what do they have in common?"

"They're all good," Clove said.

"They're also weak," I said. "Snow White doesn't save herself, the prince does. Cinderella doesn't tell her stepmother and stepsisters where to stick it, because the prince saves her. Rapunzel sits in that tower for years waiting for a man to save her. All they do is sit around and wait for someone to save them."

Landon moved his hand from mine and pulled me closer to him, resting his face against the side of my head. "I don't know what to think about that."

"I think the curse is latching on to certain parts of our personality," I said. "That's why Thistle is getting grumpier. That's why Clove is getting whinier. That's why I'm getting more ... uncertain. The longer we're here, the more our personalities are going to change."

"This is such crap," Landon said, pressing a quick kiss to my forehead. "I'm going to have to kill your Aunt Tillie. You know that, right?"

"That's probably why you're turning into a villain, like me," Thistle said.

"We need to keep moving," I said. "Any detours we take, we need to make a plan and get through them."

"Are we leaving that kid to be eaten by a wolf?" Landon asked.

"He's not real," I said. "He's not being eaten. He's not feeling pain. He's a fictional character."

"Okay," Landon said, giving in. "Let's keep moving."

As everyone turned to file back to the path Landon kept me close. "I can't turn into a villain," he murmured.

"You won't," I said. "I have faith. You're just ... emotionally charged right now."

"I feel out of control."

"We all feel out of control."

"I would never hurt you, Bay," Landon said. "You know that, right?"

"I know that."

"Marcus didn't seem to," Landon said bitterly.

"Marcus is dealing with the same thing we are," I said.

"Do you think he's becoming a villain?"

I shook my head. "He's too mellow. I think the only reason some of that stuff is starting to happen to you is because you're strong ... and bossy."

"You're bossy, too."

"Not like you and Thistle. Things will only get worse before they get better," I said.

"I love you, Bay," Landon said earnestly.

"I love you, too."

"I'm still going to kill your Aunt Tillie."

"We're all going to kill her," Thistle called from the front of the formation. "You're going to have to get in line."

"I am the line," Landon replied.

"No way ... oh, come on," Thistle said. "Get up here."

Landon and I increased our pace, and when we walked out of the woods we found a red cape hanging from a tree branch next to the path. Everything else was the same except for the new clothing item.

"Red Riding Hood," Marcus said, looking the cape up and down. "What do you think? Should we leave it here and keep going?"

"No," I said, an idea forming. "Thistle needs to put it on."

"Why me?" Thistle whined.

"Because you're becoming a villain," I said. "You need to be the hero again to ward off those inner urges of yours."

"Are you sure?"

"No," I admitted. "It's just a feeling."

"Her feelings have been right so far," Landon said. "Put it on. Maybe it will lead us to the wolf and … Daniel."

Thistle scowled. "If I get eaten by a wolf I swear I'm going to come back and haunt you for the rest of your lives." She grabbed the cloak and swung it over her shoulders, tying it around her neck before planting her feet on the brick road. "Bring it on, wolf!"

I swallowed my upper lip with my lower to keep from laughing, risking a glance at Landon, who didn't bother hiding his smile.

Thistle cocked her head to the side, waiting. "Where is it?"

"Maybe we have to keep walking," I said. "It would be anticlimactic if the wolf simply jumped out of the woods immediately and attacked you."

"I guess," Thistle said.

We picked up our trek, Thistle leading the way with Marcus close on her heels. He wasn't letting her out of his sight.

"Do you think we're going to Grandma's house?" Clove asked. "This is Aunt Tillie's story, after all. Maybe we'll finally get to meet her."

"I keep forgetting you guys never got a chance to meet your grandmother," Landon said.

"Aunt Tillie was our grandmother," I said. "Although we were told if we ever called her that we'd have our mouths glued shut for a month – and she was going to use actual glue."

Landon snickered. "That sounds like her."

He was making an effort to embrace the lighter side of things right now, visions of mustache-twirling dancing through his head as he fought to keep himself calm even though he really wanted to find the wolf that took Daniel and beat it to a pulp. I squeezed his hand reassuringly.

"You're not a villain," I said. "You're a good guy. You're the best guy."

He smiled. "You don't need to coddle me, Bay. I understand what's going on here and I'm determined to ... stop being a douche. It's going to be okay."

"That's easy for you to say," Thistle said. "You're not the one wearing the red cloak of death waiting for the wolf to jump out at you."

"I don't think it's going to jump out at you," I said, pulling up short and fixing my attention on the cabin that had mysteriously popped up along the road seconds before. "I think it's in there."

"Oh, good," Thistle said. "It's Grandmother's cabin."

"Are we all going in together?" Clove asked, nervous.

"We're not separating," I said. "Thistle is taking the lead, and you and Sam can take up the rear if you want, but we're all going in there."

"Fine," Clove said. "I just don't want to fight a wolf."

"Don't worry," Thistle said. "I think I'm going to be the one fighting the wolf." She sucked in a breath and then veered off the road, heading straight for the cabin. When she got to the door she paused long enough to shoot me a look. "Do I knock?"

"I have no idea," I said. "Does proper etiquette even exist in fairy tales? The bears said I climbed right in their beds."

"Good point." Thistle turned the handle and threw open the door with as much dramatic flair as she could muster. "Grandma, I'm home!"

Clove giggled. "I think she's having fun."

She certainly looked as though she was enjoying herself.

Thistle stepped into the cabin boldly. "Where are you, Grandma?"

The replying voice was almost comical. It sounded as if a drunken trucker was trying to play a soap opera heroine. "I'm in here, dear."

"Great," Thistle said. "Just ... hold on. I'll be right there."

We followed Thistle into the cabin and watched her scan the room. Finally, she strode to the fireplace and grabbed a metal poker, testing its weight before squaring her shoulders and facing the back of the cabin. A simple sheet closed it off from the rest of the cabin. We all knew what we would find in there when Thistle pulled back the sheet.

"Hit it fast," Landon whispered. "Don't give it time to talk."

AMANDA M. LEE

"This is my fairy tale," Thistle said. "I haven't gotten to see any animals talk yet. Let me have a little fun. The Goddess knows we could use it."

"Let her go," I said.

"Fine," Landon said. "If you take too long, though, I'm going to step in and handle things my way."

"You usually do," Thistle said. She moved to the sheet and pulled it to the side, her face a mask of faux enthusiasm when she faced the bed occupant.

This world was full of odd things, but the sight of a wolf in a nightgown and nightcap, spectacles perched on its long snout, was almost more than I could take. It was like a bad sitcom. All we were missing was the laugh track.

"Hi, Grandma," Thistle said. "How are you today?"

"I'm just fine, dear," the wolf said. "Although ... I am a little weak. You should move closer so I can get a better look at you."

"I'm good here," Thistle said. "You smell like you've been in that bed for a long time, and I'm afraid of bed bugs. They freak me out."

The wolf was flummoxed. "But ... I want to see you."

"You're not missing anything," Thistle said, glancing around the makeshift sick room. "I look the same as I did the last time you saw me. I might be a little sweatier ... and dirtier ... but I'm pretty much the same."

"I want to give you a hug," the wolf said.

"I'm afraid of personal contact, so I'm going to have to pass on that," Thistle said. "Hugs make me feel all wonky, like you're trying to invade my personal space. I told you that last time I was here. Don't you remember?"

"I ... well ... of course," the wolf said. "It's just that I like to hug."

"You'll survive," Thistle said. "So, Grandma, what did you do today?"

"I ... um ... just laid in bed," the wolf said. "That's what I usually do."

"No, you don't," Thistle said, embracing her role. "You usually knit for a few hours, and then you read some of those torrid bodice-rippers you love so much. Oh, and you like to shave your legs while you're in bed, too. Can I see if you did that today?"

The wolf frowned. "I ... no! What's wrong with you?"

"What's wrong with you?" Thistle asked. "You don't look like the grandmother I usually visit. In fact, if I didn't know better, I would say you're an imposter."

"I'm not an imposter," the wolf squeaked. "I'm your grandmother."

Thistle arched an eyebrow. "Really? When's my birthday?"

"I forgot."

"What's my mother's name?"

"Mom?"

"Close," Thistle said. "Try again."

"Mommy?"

"Okay, enough is enough," Landon said. "You're wasting time. Kill it and let's get going."

"You always have to ruin my fun," Thistle grumbled.

"You're the only one having fun."

"Oh, whatever." Thistle whipped the fireplace poker from behind her back and brandished it in front of the wolf. "Where is Daniel?"

"Who is Daniel? What are you going to do with that?"

"I'm going to stab you with it," Thistle replied.

"But ... I'm your grandmother."

"You're a wolf in a nightgown," Thistle said. "Who falls for this act, by the way?"

"Hey, this isn't how this is supposed to go," the wolf said, lapsing into a deeper voice and glancing around the room. "You're supposed to come in and fall for my act. You're supposed to comment on my eyes and nose ... and I'm supposed to get more and more menacing ... and then you're supposed to scream while I eat you."

"That's not how the story ends," Thistle said. "You get killed by ... who does kill the wolf in that story? Is it the woodsman?"

"That sounds right," I said. "I don't remember."

"This is all wrong," the wolf said, shaking his head hard enough that the spectacles slipped down his snout. "You can't change the story. That's not how this works. You have to follow the script."

"I don't have to do anything," Thistle said. "This is my story. It became my story the second I put the cloak on. I can end it any way I want."

"I want to see the author," the wolf said, crossing his paws over his chest. "This is not the role I signed on for."

"None of us signed on for this," Thistle said, plunging the poker into the wolf's chest. "We still have to play the game."

The wolf howled the second the poker hit his chest. Instead of creating a wound, though, the poker detonated the wolf into a cloud of confetti over the bed. The cabin dissolved around us, and we were back on the yellow brick road.

"Wow," Clove said. "That was cool."

"It was also educational," I said. "That wolf knew it was in a story."

"We also found we can change the script," Thistle said. "That means we should be able to work our way through these stories a lot faster than we have been. Every story book character we find we just have to kill."

"I think that's taking things a little far," Landon said. "What if you could only kill the wolf because it was a villain?"

"Oh, good point," Thistle said. "Okay, new plan. Every villain we come across we need to kill. Every hero we come across we need to ask a few questions and then keep going. Every victim we come across … I'm sorry Landon … we have to ignore them."

I was worried Landon would disagree, but when I turned to him he was already nodding his head in agreement. "That's the plan. Let's move, people. There might finally be some light at the end of this tunnel."

Never take candy from strangers. There's probably something wrong with it. The only exception is a Snickers. Go ahead and take it then, but don't eat it. Bring it back for me, and I'll test it for you.

– *Aunt Tillie's Wonderful World of Stories to Make Little Girls Shut Up*

CHAPTER 11

"I kind of miss the cloak," Thistle said.

We'd been walking about twenty minutes, and instead of the pall that had been following us for what felt like hours, we were feeling markedly lighter.

"I miss food," Clove said.

My stomach rumbled in agreement. "I do, too."

"I'm guessing there's no food in fairy land," Landon said, rubbing his own stomach sadly. "I would kill for a bacon cheeseburger right now."

"I wouldn't trust the food here," Thistle said. "We know the apples are poisonous."

"Maybe it's just the apples," I suggested.

"Do you want to take that chance?"

She had a point. "I guess not."

We walked on for a few minutes, silent. My stomach refused to quit growling, though, and Landon's was starting to rumble in tandem with mine. "Now that Clove brought up food that's all I can think about," I said.

"Me, too," Thistle said. "If you can believe it, I swear I smell pot roast."

I sniffed the air, groaning when I realized her words carried the power of suggestion. "Now I can, too. Thanks so much."

"You're not the only one," Sam said. "I think I can smell baked ham. It smells just like my mom's kitchen. She used to make a big one for Sunday dinner once a month, and then we would have something to make sandwiches with for days. It was amazing."

"I smell French fries," Marcus said. "Not only can I smell the fries, I can smell the salt."

I glanced at Landon. "Let me guess, you smell bacon?"

He smiled, rueful. "Am I that transparent?"

"You're predictable in your love of bacon," I said. "I think, if it came down to it, you'd choose bacon over me."

"Never," Landon said. "I would choose to have you wrap yourself in bacon, though."

"You're so sick."

"You're both sick," Thistle said. "I … hey … what's that?"

We moved to her side, our gazes sliding in the direction she pointed. What we saw was straight out of a fantasy – one we'd all been living in mere seconds before.

"Is that what I think it is?" Landon asked, leaning forward.

"It's a cottage," Clove said.

"I don't care about the cottage," Landon said. "I'm talking about the garden. It looks as if it's made out of … food."

"Let's see," Thistle said, skipping off the road and heading toward the cottage.

"Thistle, be careful," Marcus warned. "This could be a trap."

"Of course it's a trap," Thistle said. "It's Hansel and Gretel's story."

I froze, her words bringing the old tale to focus. Of course.

"Hansel and Gretel were tempted by a cottage made of gingerbread and candy," Clove said. "This is a cottage made of … oh, man, is that flower pot full of burritos? I love burritos!"

"This is still a cottage dreamed up by Aunt Tillie," I said. "She likes candy, but she likes regular food more. This would be her idea of a dream getaway."

"It's my idea of a dream getaway, too," Landon said, moving closer to the cottage. "Look, sweetie, there's bacon big enough to wrap yourself in here." He waggled an eyebrow suggestively.

"I'm glad you're feeling better."

"Me, too."

I followed him, keeping close. My eyes couldn't help but widen as each new garden entrée came into view. All of Aunt Tillie's favorites – and most of mine – were here.

"Oh, there's pot roast and barbecue ribs and prime rib and a big Thanksgiving turkey," Thistle said. "I need to eat!"

My mouth watered and my mind went fuzzy as I reached for a fried chicken leg, and then something sounded in the back of my brain. It was a warning. "Wait."

No one listened. Landon's hands reached for a pinwheel made of bacon slices. It was almost as if he couldn't hear me.

"Wait!"

Everyone froze, hands outstretched, eyes glassy.

"The food is cursed," I said. "We can't eat it."

"I'm not sure I care," said Sam, rubbing his hands over the top of a glazed ham as though he was about to propose to it.

"You're going to care if it prolongs how long we're in here," I said. "In the story the candy is drugged. That means this food is probably drugged. We can't eat it."

"I'm so hungry, though," Clove whined.

"It's not as though we're starving here," I said. "We ate at the inn a few hours ago. We stuffed ourselves silly. We can't eat this." I turned to Landon, pleading. "We can't."

Landon found the control he was missing and stepped away from the bacon. "Bay is right. We can't eat this."

"Speak for yourself," Thistle said, reaching for a hamburger daisy and plucking it from the stem. "Aunt Tillie loves food. She's not going to poison it ... even in a book. She would consider that sacrilegious."

"I'm with Thistle," Marcus said, grabbing a bouquet of French fry posies and taking one from the center. "This is going to be good. It's going to be fine." He popped one of the fries in his mouth, chewing enthusiastically. "See."

AMANDA M. LEE

"That's good enough for me," Thistle said, biting into the hamburger. "I knew Aunt Tillie wouldn't poison the food. Some things are forever, and that's exactly what Aunt Tillie's love of food is."

Marcus reached for a second French fry, but before he could pop it into his mouth he tilted forward and crashed to the ground, his bouquet of fries scattering across the green grass.

Thistle swallowed hard, her gaze falling on Marcus. "What just happened? Did he pass out because he was so hungry?"

Thistle barely got the words out before she dropped her burger and fell to the ground next to Marcus.

I stormed over to them, checking them both to make sure they had a pulse, and then straightened. "Does anyone else want to eat the food?"

"I think I just lost my appetite," Sam said.

"Me, too," Clove said, horrified. "Are they alive?"

"They're sleeping," I said. I rubbed my forehead and glanced at Landon. "Are you okay?"

"You saved me," he said, breaking into a wide grin. "Maybe you're the prince."

"That's going to make our sex life really creepy," I pointed out.

"You're right," Landon conceded. "You can be a modern princess. I'd especially like it if you ditched the frilly dresses and embraced latex."

I couldn't help but smile. It didn't last long, but it felt good. "We have a new problem obviously," I said, gesturing toward Marcus and Thistle's prone bodies. "Now we have to solve this story to get those two back on their feet."

"I don't know what I remember about this story," Landon said. "My mother wasn't big on fairy tales. Doesn't a witch live in that cottage?"

"Yes. She drugs the candy – or in this case burgers and fries – and then captures the children so she can eat them."

"Nice," Landon said. "If I hadn't already lost my appetite, that would have pretty much killed it."

"How does the witch in the story die?" Sam asked.

"The kids turn the tables on her when she's not looking and push her in the oven and roast her alive," I said.

"Have you ever considered how violent these stories are?" Clove asked, wrinkling her nose. "I mean, think about it. The wolf tries to eat Little Red Riding Hood. The witch poisons Snow White. This witch tries to eat children. It's really pretty ... awful."

"It is," I agreed. "We don't have time to talk about that now, though. If you want to debate the merits of fairy tales, I'll be happy to do it for hours on end – over pizza and chocolate martinis – once we're back in the guesthouse."

"We have to go in the cottage, right?" Landon asked.

"We do," I said.

"Are we all going?" Clove was nervous again. "I think that only two of us should go. That way someone will be out here to watch Marcus and Thistle and, if the first couple fails, there will be another couple to save them."

She was so transparent. "I'm guessing you want to be the one to watch over Thistle and Marcus."

"I'm more nurturing, so that probably makes sense."

I rolled my eyes until they landed on Landon. "Do you want to kill a witch with me?"

"Sure," he said. "It might be a nice way to get out some of my aggression so I don't really murder Aunt Tillie when we get out of here."

"Let's go," I said, gesturing toward the door. "I want to get this over with ... mainly because I want to make sure Thistle admits I was right and she was wrong."

"That's a beautiful trait, sweetie," Landon said, pressing his hand against the small of my back as he ushered me toward the cottage. "It really turns me on."

"Are you joking?"

"Actually I'm not," Landon said. "If you toss in a little dance while you do the 'I'm right' song I'll reward you with a romantic dinner at the seafood restaurant of your choice when we get out of this."

"Really?"

"All the crab legs you can eat."

"I really do love that you get me," I said.

He kissed my cheek quickly. "Me, too. Come on. Let's fry a witch." He snorted. "We should start making a list of the things I say tonight. They could make a really funny book."

"I'll try to remember." I raised my hand to knock and then thought better of it. "I'm thinking we should use the element of surprise here. What do you think?"

"Let's break the law, baby."

I turned the handle quietly, carefully pushing the door open. A cursory glance around the room told me that this witch had horrible taste. It was as though she had a subscription to *Better Homes and Gardens* and instead of picking one theme she picked every theme and crammed it into the same room. This witch was a crazy hoarder. At least I didn't see one hundred cats. That would have only made the situation worse.

"This is unbelievably tacky," Landon said.

"Shouldn't you have been tipped off by the potluck yard?"

"That was beautiful."

The sound of footsteps on hardwood floors grabbed our attention. The woman who walked into the room was dressed in a hideous floor-length Victorian gown, a high lace neck covering her throat. Her gray hair was piled on top of her head, and other than some unnaturally saggy skin she looked relatively normal.

"You must be … ." Landon broke off, unsure. "Do I just call you Mrs. Witch?"

"Who are you and what are you doing in my house?"

I couldn't contain my surprise when I recognized the woman. It had been years since I had seen her. The last time was at a summer camp when she came to pick up her nasty granddaughter, Rosemary. That was fourteen years ago, though. It just couldn't be. "Aunt Willa?"

"Do I know you?" The woman seemed surprised by my recognition.

"Who is she?" Landon asked.

"She's Aunt Tillie's sister."

"I thought your grandmother was Aunt Tillie's sister."

"She had two sisters," I said.

"What happened to the second one? Did she die, too?"

"No," I said. "She was just kind of ... banished from the family." I forced a tight smile onto my face as I regarded my great-aunt, who was, if you can believe it, even worse than the great-aunt who cursed us into a book of children's stories. "How are you, Aunt Willa?"

"I don't know you," Aunt Willa said, crossing her arms over her chest. "Why do you keep speaking to me as if you know me?"

"She's not real, Bay," Landon said. "She's not your aunt."

He was right. Instinctively I knew it. It was so surreal to think about. I cleared my throat. "You bear a resemblance to someone I know," I said. "I'm sorry for the mistake."

"That doesn't explain why you're in my house," Aunt Willa said. "When you enter someone's house you're supposed to knock. There wasn't any knocking. I would have heard it."

"We're sorry," Landon said. "We got lost in the woods. We're looking for a ... phone."

"A what?"

"There are no phones here," I said. "Actually, we're looking for a glass of water. We're really thirsty."

"You expect me to reward you for breaking into my house?"

She may have been a figment of Aunt Tillie's colorful imagination, but she was exactly as I remembered her. I'd hated her visits when I was a child – and not only because she always brought my second cousin Rosemary with her. Rosemary was such an awful person. Aunt Willa taught Rosemary how to be evil, and Rosemary had nothing on her beloved grandmother.

"You're right," I said. "We don't deserve water." I glanced around the cottage, my eyes falling on a heavy-looking book.

"Get out of my house," Aunt Willa commanded.

"Actually, we were hoping you would show us your cottage," Landon said. "We're looking to buy a house, and we love this one."

"It's not for sale."

AMANDA M. LEE

"We'll offer you a lot of money. Just let us see the kitchen." Landon winked, trying to charm her.

"I said 'no,'" Aunt Willa said. "Now, if you don't get out of my house, you're not going to like what happens."

"Are you going to eat us?" All his charm was gone. Now Landon was irritated. "Isn't that what you do? You lure children here with a yard full of yummy goodies, you drug them, you cook them and then you eat them."

"I don't always cook them," Aunt Willa sneered.

Landon made a face. "That's even grosser."

"Well, you're out of luck," Aunt Willa said. "I only like … young meat. You're too old."

"We're not here to be eaten," Landon said. "We're here to … Bay, do you want to help me out here?"

"Sure," I said. "What the heck is that?" I practically screamed the question and pointed. When Aunt Willa swiveled to see what I pointing at, I grabbed the book and brought it down on the back of her head as hard as I could, knocking her out. She tumbled to the floor, landing hard.

"That was nice," Landon said. "I thought we had to cook her, though?"

"I was hoping we could bypass that little tidbit," I said. "Since she didn't poof into confetti like the wolf, though, I'm guessing we're going to have to play it all out."

"Great," Landon said, hooking Aunt Willa under her arms and grimacing as he lifted her. "Go turn the oven on."

WELL, that was the grossest thing I've ever done," I said, wiping my hands on my jeans and moving away from the oven. "Let's get out of here."

"Don't we have to wait … and watch?"

"I don't think that's necessary," I said, leading Landon from the kitchen and back into the living room.

It had taken us almost twenty minutes to load Aunt Willa into the oven. Folding her in there was a lot harder than we thought. After trying three different configurations, we finally got her settled and closed the door. Now we waited for the final act to play out.

"Go look out on the front lawn," I said. "I'll keep an eye on the door in case she somehow manages to climb out of there. The second you see Marcus and Thistle get to their feet we can go."

"And you can do your song and dance," Landon said, laughing.

"Exactly."

Landon gave me a light kiss and shuffled to the door. He leaned out so he could scan the yard. "Not yet."

I turned back to the kitchen, focusing on the oven door, which I could barely see from my vantage point. A loud bang reverberated from the adjacent room. I could only hope that wasn't Aunt Willa coming to in the oven.

"They're moving," Landon said.

"She probably poofed into confetti in there," I said. "That's probably what I heard."

Landon didn't reply. I turned my attention from the kitchen and found an empty room. The doorway was vacant ... and I was alone. "Landon?"

I started moving toward the door, the room dissolving behind me. Once everything was gone, instead of being within walking distance of the familiar brick road I found myself in a dark room. There was no sign of Landon. Clove and Sam weren't standing on the lawn waiting for Marcus and Thistle to regain their senses. I was really and truly alone.

I jumped when I heard the sound of voices, hoping everyone else was transported here with me.

"Cinderella!"

"Oh, crap," I said. "Why me?"

No one can make you do something you don't want to do unless you let them. Except me. Always do what I tell you to do. I'm always right, and you'll regret it if you cross me.

– *Aunt Tillie's Wonderful World of Stories to Make Little Girls Shut Up*

CHAPTER 12

"Landon," I hissed, scanning the dimly lit room and trying to hold off the settling panic.

He didn't answer.

"This isn't helping my abandonment issues," I grumbled, wiping my hand down my hips and frowning as I glanced down. My jeans and T-shirt were gone, replaced by a set of filthy rags that made my skin crawl. It was a dress – barely – tattered at the hem and hanging off my shoulders. A quick look down the bodice told me that bras were apparently banned in this tale. "Double crap."

"Cinderella!"

I pressed my eyes shut, irritation and worry warring for supremacy in my mind. This couldn't be happening. Not only had I been transported into my least favorite fairy tale, I also was the character who was about to be utilized for slave labor. I can't even keep up on my own laundry.

"There you are." The voice was like nails on a chalkboard, and I recognized it instantly when the slim figure stepped into the doorway of the dirty room. I guess it was supposed to be a kitchen, but without a microwave and Keurig I couldn't be sure. "Have you been hiding here all morning?"

My high school nemesis, Lila Stevens, fixed me with a harsh look, and I had to bite my tongue to keep from unleashing hours of frustration on her. In my head, I knew the character only looked like Lila. It wasn't really her. In my heart, though, I still hated her. It couldn't be a coincidence that Lila was appearing in this specific story. "I'm not hiding," I said. "I'm ... contemplating the meaning of life."

"Oh, whatever," Lila said, stepping into the room. She wrinkled her nose disdainfully. "This place smells ... and you smell. You should try taking a bath."

"You should try shutting your mouth," I grumbled, brushing my hair from my face. It felt greasy. That couldn't be good.

"What did you just say to me?" Lila flounced down the stairs, stopping right in front of me. Her hands were on her narrow waist, which looked thinner than normal thanks to the corset and hoop skirt under her bright pink dress.

"I didn't say anything," I said, bartering for time. I wasn't sure what to do. "Do you need something?"

"I need my breakfast," Lila said. "You were supposed to serve it to me five minutes ago. I'm hungry."

I pointed to the pot above the open flame in the fireplace. "Go nuts."

"Excuse me?" Lila's eyes were narrow slits of seething hatred. "Are you suggesting I cook my own breakfast?"

"Or go hungry," I said. "I don't really care which. Although, to be fair, I'm guessing you'll be quiet if you have something shoved in that huge mouth of yours so I would prefer that you ate something."

"I ... I .... I ... ." Lila's mouth was open but only staccato sounds emanated. It was a nice change of pace.

"Have you seen any ... strangers ... around?" I asked.

"Strangers?"

"Three men and two women. They would probably be dressed in clothes you would find ... odd."

"I find you odd," Lila said. "You're speaking to me as though we're ... equals. We may be stepsisters, but you're not my equal. You need to learn your station in life."

"Thanks for the suggestion," I said. "Um ... where is the front door to this place? I need to get out of here. Which way is the yellow brick road?"

"What are you talking about?" a now-furious Lila asked. "Have you gone crazy? Have you lost your mind? Are you suffering from the vapors?"

"I might be going crazy," I conceded. "I'm pretty sure my mind is teetering on the edge. I have no idea what the vapors are. Is that like gas? I definitely have heartburn, which is pretty interesting since I haven't eaten in hours."

"I can't even look at you," Lila said, covering her eyes dramatically. "You're like some horrible monster."

"You're as lovely as ever," I said, pushing past her and moving toward the door. "Just give me a hint. Do I want to make a right or a left when I get out of this room? I need to get out of this place. I am not finishing this story. I hate this story."

"What story?"

"You wouldn't believe me if I told you," I replied, glancing into the hallway. There was nothing to signify which was the correct way to go. The structure was made of stone, high arching doorways cutting into the granite walls at regular intervals. It appeared to be a sort of castle, but I couldn't be sure. "So ... right? Left?"

"I'm telling," Lila said, shoving past me and taking a hard right. "You're going to be in so much trouble you won't be able to walk when Mama is done taking the switch to you."

Mama? Ugh. Who did Aunt Tillie cast in that role in her little fantasy world? It couldn't be good. Despite my better judgment, I followed Lila down the long hallway. If I could just find a way to get outside of this place I could walk until I found the yellow brick road – and my family.

"Mama!"

I rolled my eyes. Lila was even more annoying in this world. At least I knew she was behind bars in the real world. She was allowed to run around willy-nilly here. Life just isn't fair sometimes.

"Mama!"

Lila's long corkscrew curls swung vigorously as she stomped down the hallway. I had an incredible urge to yank one of them. I had no idea why.

"Mama!"

"Why are you screeching?"

Another figure popped into view from one of the doorways. It took me a second, and a bevy of unhappy memories from my childhood, to recognize her. I didn't think this was Mama. This had to be the other stepsister. Even though she didn't look exactly the same – a little more weight spreading around her hips than I remembered throwing me – years couldn't erase the pinched and unpleasant face of .... "Rosemary."

Rosemary tucked a strand of dirty blonde hair behind her ear. Unlike Lila's bouncy curls, lifeless hanks that looked as though they hadn't encountered a brush in years marked Rosemary's locks.

"Where is our breakfast, Cinderella?"

"It's in the pot in the kitchen," I said. "Which way is the door? I need to get out of here."

"How are we supposed to eat it if it's in the kitchen?"

"I would suggest using a spoon," I said. "Or, in your case, maybe a shovel."

Rosemary was as flummoxed as Lila. "Is this supposed to be some kind of joke?"

"While I'm sure you go through life with people laughing every time they see you, I can assure you this isn't a joke," I said. "Now, where is the door?"

"I'm telling Mama," Rosemary said, placing her hands on her wide hips and glowering at me. "You're going to be in so much trouble you won't know what hit you."

"Whatever," I said. "I need to find the door. Where is it?"

"Mama!"

Rosemary's voice was even more annoying than Lila's. Nails on a chalkboard would be a reprieve.

"What are you two screeching about?"

I swiveled quickly, my gaze landing on another familiar figure from my life. This one was ... jarring. "Edith?"

Edith was the resident ghost at The Whistler, the Hemlock Cove newspaper where I worked. She'd been haunting the offices since she keeled over at her desk decades earlier. I'd never known her as anything other than a phantom presence. Seeing her whole – blood pounding through her veins – was fascinating.

"What's going on?" Edith asked. "Why is everyone yelling?"

"I can't believe you're ... real," I said, touching her shoulder. "Well, I know you're not real. I can actually touch you, though. It's ... so different. Do you feel different?"

"Are you somehow addled?" Edith jerked her shoulder from my probing finger. "Have you forgotten your station in this house?"

I guess, in a weird way, it made sense for Aunt Tillie to turn Edith into a nasty stepmother. She'd always had a problem with the woman in life, constantly complaining that Edith was trying to steal Uncle Calvin from her. I had no idea whether that was true, but Aunt Tillie's dislike of Edith was legendary. It was dwarfed only by her dislike of Aunt Willa, Rosemary and Lila. I shouldn't have expected anything else when Aunt Tillie decided to paint a picture of otherworldly villains.

"Um ... I'm guessing I'm your personal house slave," I said. "The thing is, I have to ... meet some people. I can't make your breakfast this morning. You're on your own."

Edith's dark eyes fixed on me, and while she was never overly fond of me – unless she needed something – I found overt hatred there now. I inadvertently took a step back.

"Who are you meeting?" Edith asked, suspicious.

"Just some friends," I said. "We're going to a ... party."

"What party?"

"I think it has a lot in common with a pity party," I replied.

"I think you're up to something," Edith said. "I think you're going to try to sneak into the castle."

"Isn't this the castle?"

Edith ignored me. "I think you heard about the prince picking a bride tonight," she said. "Do you honestly think you have a chance with a prince? You're a servant. You'll never be anything other than a servant."

"I'm not interested in the prince," I said. "I don't particularly like princes. I'm happy with my lot in life ... which isn't here."

"Oh, I know what you're trying to do," Edith said, reaching over and grabbing my chin so I had no choice but to focus on her. "I won't let anyone mess with Rosemary and Lila's chance to snare a prince."

I jerked my chin out of her hand, grimacing when I felt her claw-like fingernails catch on my skin. "I don't care about your stupid prince. I don't care about your castle. I don't care about any of it. I just want to get out of here."

I stalked toward the far end of the hallway, hoping I could find an external door if left to my own devices for five minutes without nattering voices burrowing into the back of my brain. Things probably would have been fine if I had kept my mouth shut. That's not in my nature, though.

I turned around long enough to grace Edith with a withering look. "And neither one of your terrible daughters has a chance with the prince. Rosemary looks as though she fell off the back of the ugly truck and Lila has the personality of my ass. Neither one of them has a chance. Just ... suck it up."

TWO HOURS later I was sitting in the storage room where Edith, Rosemary and Lila locked me in after wrestling me down and ... quite frankly ... pulling my hair. My scalp hurt ... and I was really grumpy.

I was at a loss. Somewhere out there Landon was looking for me. I knew it. He was probably panicking because he couldn't find me. Or – and this was a troubling thought – he was about to start waltzing with hundreds of desperate women at the castle. What if he was the prince? I was Cinderella, after all. I was supposed to claim the prince.

"Crap," I groaned, dropping my head into my hands. "I should have killed Lila the second she walked into the kitchen."

"Well, that would have been a stupid idea. Murderers can't marry a prince."

I lifted my head when I heard the voice, my mouth dropping open at the face peering through the small window in the door. "Aunt Tillie?"

"I'm not your aunt, nincompoop," Aunt Tillie snapped. "I'm your fairy godmother."

"That's worse," I said. "You get me out of here right now!" I jumped to my feet and stormed to the door. "I can't believe you did this to us! We're your family! Do you have any idea how horrible this night has been?"

"How many times do I have to tell you that I'm not your aunt?"

"You are my aunt," I said. "You're also the narrator of this book. You trapped us in the book, and now we're stuck. You get me out of here right now!"

Aunt Tillie sighed and stepped away from the door. The lock tumbled, allowing the door to spring open, and when I strode through it I pulled up short when I saw what Aunt Tillie wore. "You're dressed up in a ... ball gown?"

It wasn't your run-of-the-mill ball gown. It was a floor-length blue monstrosity with more sequins and crystals than should be allowed by law. In addition to the dress, she carried a wand. I kind of wanted to steal it and thwack her over the head with it.

"This is how I normally dress," Aunt Tillie sniffed, crossing her arms over her chest obstinately. "I'm a fairy godmother. I always dress like this."

"I miss the camouflage and combat helmet," I snapped. "Are you ... aware of what's going on here?"

"You're Cinderella," Aunt Tillie said. "You need to go to the ball so you can snag your prince."

"I already have my prince," I said. "I just can't seem to find him right now. Do you know where he is?"

"He's at the castle."

"Are you sure?"

"I'm your fairy godmother," Aunt Tillie said. "Of course I'm sure."

I sighed, pinching the bridge of my nose as I looked to the ceiling. "What do I have to do?"

"I'm glad you asked," Aunt Tillie said, smiling. "The first thing we need is a gown."

"I can't believe this," I complained. "I hate this story. You hate this story. Why am I the one who got it? Clove is the one who would've loved this story. You should have put her here … although, I have to say, having Edith, Lila and Rosemary be the evil-doers in this one was a nice touch."

"I have no idea what you're talking about," Aunt Tillie said, brandishing her wand.

"Some of the other characters in this … book … have been self-aware," I said. "Are you?"

"I'm a fairy godmother."

I narrowed my eyes. "See, the problem is, you lie," I said. "You've always lied. You tell us what you feel like telling us as if it's truth, even though we all know it's a load of crap. Is that what you're doing now?"

"Do you want to find your prince or not?" Aunt Tillie was getting irritated. Some things never change. "I don't have all day. I have six more downtrodden women to get to before I can have a bottle of wine and relax. You're really slowing me down."

I decided to try one more thing. "Are you aware of what's going on in the real world?"

"This is the real world."

"If we die here … do we die there?" It was an ominous question, but I needed to know.

Aunt Tillie shrugged, noncommittal. "It all depends on what you believe. Now … stand over there … I'm on a bit of a timetable and you need a coach and a footman before I can get out of here. *Fairy Tale Jeopardy* starts in two hours. I can't miss it."

One day your prince will come. He's not going to put a glass slipper on your foot. He's going to be bossy and willful. He's also going to expect you to cook. Make sure you burn the first few dinners so you can keep his expectations low. If you're lucky, though, he'll also make you laugh. Make sure to keep him if he makes you laugh.

– Aunt Tillie's Wonderful World of Stories to Make Little Girls Shut Up

CHAPTER 13

"How far is the palace?"

The footman who ushered me into my carriage – which left a little to be desired since it actually smelled like a rotting pumpkin – was the quiet sort. He hadn't said a word since we left Edith's manor. It had been only three minutes, but it was an uncomfortable three minutes.

"It's right here." The footman directed the horses to the side of the road and pulled to a stop.

"Where?"

The footman pointed, and after serious study a palace began to take shape in the mist. It was beautiful. It looked like it came straight out of a ... well, a fairy tale ... but I was still irritated. "Are you really telling me I couldn't just walk the hundred and fifty feet here? This is ridiculous. Now I smell like pumpkin."

The footman opened the carriage door and extended his hand to help me out. I gathered the wide skirt of the white dress, grimacing as I tried to keep the uncomfortable glass slippers on as I descended the slippery steps.

"Thanks," I said, dropping the skirt and frowning. Now I understood how embarrassed Thistle was wearing a dress that constantly made noise. "Which way do I go?"

"I have no idea."

"Are you going to sit here and wait for me to dance with the prince and then flee before midnight, leaving a glass shoe on the ground and a dumbfounded man in my wake? If so, you can go."

"I have no intention of staying," the footman said.

"What are you going to do?"

"Well, up until five minutes ago I was a dog," the footman said. "I'd like to go back to playing with my bone."

I was overwhelmed with the mad inclination to laugh, but refrained. "Knock yourself out," I said, fighting the urge to grimace when the footman started scratching his head. Great. With my luck he was infested with fleas.

I followed the steady stream of excited guests, not missing the fact that women outnumbered men by a large margin. Most of the men were older, and I guessed they were expectant fathers trying to unload desperate daughters. The whole mating ritual was annoying.

I've never understood the Cinderella story. Don't get me wrong, I like the talking mice. They're fun. I just don't get why Cinderella didn't tell her stepmother and stepsisters to "suck it" and move out. I don't get how a man spent one dance with a woman and thought he was in love with her. I never understood why a glass slipper was so cool because, let me tell you something, they're uncomfortable and they pinch. I would trade these stupid glass slippers for a pair of Converse without thinking twice about it.

I tuned in to some of the conversation as I climbed the expansive front steps of the palace. It was mindless … and tedious. I wished Thistle was with me. Her snarky commentary would make all of this palatable. I realized it wasn't only Landon I missed; I missed my cousins, too.

"Have you ever seen the prince in person? I hear he's quite handsome."

"I hear he has hair like a beautiful god."

"I hear his teeth sparkle when he smiles."

"I hear you can see everything when he wears his dress tights."

I couldn't help but smile at the visual. Were they talking about Landon? Had he been forced into tights? That might be kind of fun to see.

The walk to the ballroom was long, and since I wasn't in the mood to get to know any of these women, I made it in silence. I was desperate for a friendly face – one that was real and not forced into a fairy tale role for a change would definitely be welcome.

Once I made it to the ballroom I scanned the sea of faces, hopeful. With each passing minute that hope faded. Clove and Thistle weren't here. Maybe this was a story for Landon and me only. I couldn't wait to see him.

"Do you see the prince?"

I arched an eyebrow as one of the other women approached me, her canary yellow dress nearly blinding me. "Um … no."

"I'm Pumpernickel."

"Bay."

"That's a strange name," Pumpernickel said. "Were you embarrassed by it growing up?"

"Well, Pumpernickel, I've never really given it much thought," I said, reaching for a finger sandwich. "So, what do you know about this prince? Is he supposed to be a good guy or a douche?"

Pumpernickel's round face was bland as she regarded me. "He's the prince."

"I realize that," I said. "I just want to know what his personality is like. Is he bossy? Does he have a hero complex? Does he have long black hair and a killer rear end … err, I mean smile?"

Pumpernickel was confused. "He's the prince."

Well, this conversation as going nowhere. "Okay."

"What I'm saying is that it doesn't matter what his personality is like," she said. "He's the prince. He's going to be the king. That's all the matters."

"That's not all that matters," I countered. "That doesn't matter at all. That's the life he was born to lead. I want to know who he is."

"He's the prince."

I was done here. "I ... ."

"Excuse me. Am I interrupting?"

Pumpernickel's face turned an unnatural shade of red. "Oh ... my ... ."

I pursed my lips and swiveled, expecting to find a waiter. If he happened to have some liquor on him I wasn't going to turn up my nose. The man behind me was handsome but generic looking. He wore a white dress coat and black pants, and he stood as if he had Aunt Tillie's wand shoved in a very uncomfortable orifice. "Oh, hey," I said. "Does whiskey exist in this world? I could definitely use a double on the rocks. Throw a lime in there, too. I'm feeling a little peckish."

The waiter smiled. "I see. You want whiskey?"

"What are you doing?" Pumpernickel hissed.

"I'm hoping to get a buzz on," I said. "That's the only thing that's going to liven up this party."

"I don't believe we have whiskey for guests," the waiter said. "It's considered a ... vagabond's drink."

"I just met her," Pumpernickel said. "We're not together."

I rolled my eyes. "What do you have? Vodka? Gin? I would kill for a chocolate martini."

"I can ask," the waiter said. "Most guests don't order off the menu at royal balls." The smile he sent me was small but inquisitive. "What house are you from?"

"Oh, um, the one next door."

"The Markham residence?"

I had no idea. "Sure."

"Are you related to Rosemary and Lila?"

"Technically, Rosemary is a second cousin," I said. "Lila is just a nightmare."

Pumpernickel fanned herself worriedly, gesturing wildly with her other hand. I had no idea what she was trying to tell me.

"You speak very ... frankly," the waiter said.

"So I've been told," I said. "You should meet my cousin Thistle. She's a lot more frank than me."

"And where is she this evening?"

"Probably bitterly bitching while walking down the yellow brick road," I said.

"Is that in this kingdom?"

I shrugged. "I'm not sure where anything is right now," I said. "Speaking of that, where is this prince? We need to get this show on the road."

The waiter smiled while Pumpernickel made mewling sounds in the back of her throat.

"You've never seen the prince?"

"Nope," I said. "I hear he's handsome, though."

"I've heard that, too."

"Shouldn't he be here by now? Isn't he supposed to dance with everyone and make his choice?"

"He is," the waiter said.

As if on cue, the music started and I shifted my attention to the dance floor. Everyone retreated from it, creating a circle. It was more fun when they did it in *Footloose*.

"Where is he?" I asked. When I turned back to the waiter he was watching me with a wide smile and extended hand. "Shall we?"

"I thought only the prince was supposed to dance," I said.

"He is."

"Won't you get in trouble?"

"Not if I'm the prince."

Oh, holy crap. I'd been expecting Landon to be the prince. Of course it wouldn't be that easy. I ran my tongue over my teeth, embarrassed. "You're the prince?"

"That's what they tell me," the man said. "You may call me Reginald."

Of course. I shifted a look in Pumpernickel's direction. "That's what you were trying to tell me, wasn't it?"

"It's a good thing you're pretty," she said. "You're extremely stupid."

"That's what I hear." I had no idea what to do. For lack of a better idea, and because every eye on in the room was trained on me, I took Reginald's hand and let him lead me to the dance floor.

Thankfully, because this was a fairy tale, Reginald was a perfect gentleman when he put his hand to the small of my back and began leading me around the dance floor. He seemed to be enjoying himself. I was thankful I could get this dance out of the way before slipping away.

"Are you visiting your cousin?"

"Unfortunately."

"You don't seem to like your family," Reginald said, his eyes twinkling. "May I ask why?"

"I love my family," I said. "I'm not particularly fond of one member of it right now, but in general I love them. Edith, Rosemary and Lila aren't my family, though."

"But you said ... ."

"It's a long story," I said. "I can't explain it."

"I'm a good listener."

"Um ... that's okay."

Reginald spun me around the dance floor a few more times, the silence stifling as he wracked his brain for conversation. When the song ended, I expected him to release me and move on. Instead, he kept me close and immediately started dancing again when the new song started up.

"I thought you were only supposed to dance with each woman once?"

"Until I find the woman I like," Reginald replied, grinning. "I've already found mine."

Uh-oh. "You don't even know me."

"What do I need to know?" Reginald twirled me out wide and then pulled me back as I tried to escape. "You're beautiful – the most beautiful woman in the room, in fact. You're wise. You say odd things. You don't fear me. You're perky. You're perfect."

"I'm not perfect," I said, my voice rising an octave. "I'm pretty far from perfect."

"Not to me."

"You have no idea how much work I am," I said. "I'm insecure. I'm whiny. I hate mornings. I don't like cleaning. In the mornings, my hair looks as if it had been through a wind tunnel. I snore. I get irritated for no particular reason. Oh, and three days out of every month I'm unbearable."

Reginald smiled. He opened his mouth to respond but was cut off when another figure moved in behind him and tapped him on the shoulder. "May I cut in?"

I almost cried in relief when I saw Landon. He was still dressed in his regular clothes, and even though he looked out of place at the ball I'd never been happier to see anyone in my entire life. "Landon!"

He shot me a reassuring smile and then focused back on Reginald. "I think you're dancing with my date," he said.

"Your date?" Reginald arched an eyebrow. "This is my ball. All of these women are my dates."

"Well, that sounds … greedy," Landon said. "How about we make a deal? You can have all the other women in the room and I'll take only this one off your hands."

"I want this woman," Reginald countered. "You can have the rest of them."

"I can only handle one," Landon said. "This one."

"She's mine," Reginald replied. "I'm the prince. I get to pick my princess. I want her."

"She's already my princess," Landon said, gritting his teeth and forcing his face to remain placid. "I've already claimed her."

"Then why is she here?" Reginald pressed.

"She didn't have much of a choice," Landon said. "I'm here to … rescue her."

"But she's mine," Reginald said.

"Listen, pal, stop saying that," Landon snapped. "She's my princess. Mine." He thumped his chest for emphasis. "We were separated a couple of hours ago, and I've been going crazy trying to find her. Now, I know this whole dog-and-pony show is important to you, but this princess already has a prince. Pick someone else."

"I want this princess," Reginald said, stubbornly pulling me closer to him. "She's mine."

"I'm going to have to punch him," Landon warned. "I'm not joking. I don't have much of a sense of humor right now. I almost freaked out when that cottage dissolved and you were gone. I … I thought I lost you."

My heart rolled at the admission. "I had a minor freakout myself when I found myself in a dirty kitchen. You'll never guess who my stepmother was."

Landon waited, feigning patience.

"Edith. She was real. I could touch her. Rosemary and Lila were my stepsisters, too. It was awful."

Landon made a face. "That sounds awful."

"How did you know where to find me?" I asked, resisting Reginald as he tried to continue the dance.

"We were walking down the road because we didn't know what else to do and then this castle … suddenly it was there and we knew," Landon said. He reached out for me. "Come on. Let's get out of here."

Reginald jerked me away from Landon forcefully. "She's mine!"

"That did it." Landon cocked his fist back and slammed it into Reginald's face. The force was enough to topple the puffed-up prince, and he crumpled to the floor at our feet. Landon barely glanced at him as he stepped over the prostrate prince and pulled me in for a hug. "I was really worried, Bay."

"I thought you were going to be the prince," I admitted. "That's the only reason I came to the ball."

"I am the prince," Landon said, smiling as he ran his finger down my cheek. "You scared me." He gave me a soft kiss.

"Stop that right now," Reginald howled. "This is not how this is supposed to go. I'm the prince! I am. I get to pick my princess. I want her."

"You'll live," Landon said. "Or … well … you'll dissolve into a crying mess as soon as we're out of here. Either way, you'll be fine."

Reginald was desperate, and as Landon linked his fingers with mine and began to lead me from the dance floor he reacted in a completely dignified way (yes, I'm being sarcastic). He grabbed my leg under the dress, wrapping his fingers around my ankle, really digging in as he tried to hold on to me.

"Guards! Guards! My princess is trying to leave me!"

"That's pathetic, man," Landon said, wagging a finger in Reginald's face. "Show some manliness. You've got hundreds of women here who are begging for you to dance with them. Let the one who doesn't want you go and … suck it up. This one is mine."

"Guards! Guards!"

Landon exhaled heavily as I tried to wrench my leg from Reginald's tightening grip. "That's starting to hurt," I complained.

Landon snagged me around the waist, forcefully lifting me in his arms and dragging me away from Reginald. "Try to chill, man," Landon said. "She was never your princess to begin with."

"I got her shoe," Reginald crowed, cradling to his chest the glass slipper he'd pulled from my foot. "I got her shoe! I win!"

"Yeah, you're a real winner," Landon said. "Come on, princess. I have a few people who are anxious to see you."

If you see a beanstalk in the middle of a field, ask yourself an important question: If you have magic beans, why are you in the middle of a field? Go and sell them. Then you can go shopping. What good is a beanstalk?

– *Aunt Tillie's Wonderful World of Stories to Make Little Girls Shut Up*

CHAPTER 14

"He found you!" Clove clapped excitedly as Landon carried me back to the yellow brick road.

"We were worried," Thistle admitted, her face relaxing when our eyes met. "You look ... heavy."

"You can probably put me down now," I said, sighing. She was right. The dress had to be heavy on Landon's muscled arms. Notice I didn't say I was heavy.

"Sure," Landon said, lowering both of us to the ground next to the road and then tightening his arms around me as he settled us into a comfortable sitting configuration.

"What are you doing?" I asked, resting my forehead against his chin.

"Just ... give me a minute," Landon murmured.

"He was really worried," Clove said, her eyes wide. "He almost had a meltdown."

"Almost?" Thistle arched a challenging eyebrow. "If that was almost a meltdown, I'd hate to see the actual thing."

Landon ignored them. "I walked out of the cottage thinking everything was fine. I thought you were right behind me. When I turned around, though, the cottage and you were gone."

"Sorry about eating the food, by the way," Thistle said. "I should have listened to you."

Now I was the one challenging someone with a facial expression.

"Landon kind of let her have it when we couldn't find you," Clove explained. "He blamed getting caught in the story on Marcus and Thistle."

"Which meant it was their fault I got zapped into Cinderella's life," I said.

"How was it?" Clove asked, excited. "That dress is beautiful!"

"It's big and it's itchy," I said. "I don't understand why I'm still wearing it. We finished the story."

"Maybe you didn't learn the lesson you were supposed to," Thistle suggested. "I had to wear that pink thing for hours after my story was done."

"What lesson was I supposed to learn from this? By the way, my stepsisters were Lila and Rosemary."

"Gross," Thistle said, wrinkling her nose. "Who was your stepmother?"

"Edith."

"That's weird," Clove said.

"It kind of makes sense," Thistle said. "Aunt Tillie has always had a bug up her butt where Edith is concerned."

"Do you want to hear the craziest part?"

"It gets crazier?"

"Guess who my fairy godmother was."

Thistle pursed her lips, tilting her head to the side. "Mom?"

I shook my head.

"Your mom?"

"No. It was Aunt Tillie." Landon stirred next to me, lifting his head so he could meet my worried gaze. "Are you okay? You seem a little ... worn down."

"I thought I lost you," Landon said. "I'm fine now. Go back to the part about Aunt Tillie being your fairy godmother. Was it really her?"

"No."

"Was she self-aware, like the wolf?" Thistle asked.

"Not really," I said. "She didn't have a lot of information, and she kept telling me to shut up because she had six other girls to dress before she could watch *Fairy Tale Jeopardy*, but she didn't seem especially aware."

Landon snorted. "*Fairy Tale Jeopardy*? That's just ... great."

"She did say one interesting thing," I said. "I asked her whether we died in the real world if we died here. She kept saying this was the real world, but she added an interesting caveat. She said that it depended on what we believed."

"Does that mean if we don't believe we're going to die, we won't die?"

I shrugged. "I don't know."

Landon brushed his lips against my forehead. "Well, I choose to believe we're not going to die here. I won't let it happen. We're going to work our way through the rest of this – and it had better not take too long – and then I'm going to kill Aunt Tillie."

"I'll hold her down," Thistle grumbled.

"Did you guys come across any other stories while I was locked in a closet?"

Landon furrowed his forehead. "Why were you locked in a closet?"

I told him the story, and when I was done the laugh escaping his mouth shook his whole body. "Well, that sounds fun!"

"Then I'm telling it wrong," I said.

"We did have one story while you were gone," Clove said. "It wasn't a long one, though."

"What was it?"

"Something about goats on a bridge with an ogre under it," Thistle said.

I couldn't help but smile at the visual. "How did you get out of it?"

"Thistle was really agitated so she kicked the ogre in his special place," Clove said. "It was a short story."

"I was aiming for his knee," Thistle said. "Who knew an ogre's equipment worked differently?"

I laughed. It felt good after the past few hours of worry. "I thought Landon was going to be the prince," I said, climbing from his lap.

"When I realized that wasn't the case, I decided to get away from Reginald by any means necessary."

"I heard your plan," Landon said, smiling as he stood and dusted off the seat of his jeans. "I especially liked the part where you told him you were unbearable for three days out of every month."

I smirked. "Sadly, that didn't seem to turn him off."

"I wonder if he's still cuddling your shoe."

"Speaking of shoes," Clove said, glancing down. "How are you going to walk without shoes?"

That was a really good question. "Maybe I should just sit here and wait for some horrible fairy tale creature to come and eat me."

"That's not going to happen," Landon said. "You can have my shoes."

"Your shoes are too big," I said. "Thank you for the offer, though. Let's start walking. Maybe my feet won't get sore because this isn't real."

"I think that's wishful thinking," Clove said.

"We'll have to see," I said. "We can't stay, and I don't know how to get out of this dress." I kicked the second glass slipper off. "I think Clove would have enjoyed this story a lot more than I did. I don't know why I got it."

"Probably because you hate it," Thistle said, falling into step behind me with Marcus at her side.

"Probably."

"Just for curiosity's sake, how were you going to get away from the prince once you found out it wasn't Landon?" Clove asked.

I chuckled. "I was going to kick him in his special place," I said, slipping my hand in Landon's. "Not that I'm not happy for the assist, but I would have been fine on my own. I'm pretty sure I didn't need to be rescued."

The moment the words left my mouth my skin started to tingle. A white mist swirled around me, and when it dissipated the heavy monstrosity of a dress was gone and my jeans, T-shirt and tennis shoes were back in place.

"There's my girl," Landon said, pushing my flyaway hair out of my face. "What did you say that ended the spell?"

"I don't know," I admitted.

"I think it was the part about you not needing to be rescued," Thistle said. "Aunt Tillie always said that was the problem with princesses. They never did anything on their own because they were always waiting for a man to come save them."

That made sense. "Well ... whatever it was ... I'm just glad to be back in my regular clothes."

"Me, too," Landon said. "Although, to be fair, that dress made me want to pick you up and carry you. I can't explain it."

"I think it was the hero complex colliding with the helpless princess syndrome," I said.

"I think it was because he missed you," Thistle teased.

"Leave him alone, Thistle," I warned. "It's been a long night."

"No, she's right," Landon said. "I missed my princess." He leaned over and gave me a soft kiss. "No more separations. I don't like it."

I couldn't help but agree. "Let's keep moving. How many stories can possibly be left?"

That was probably the wrong question to ask. I'm fairly sure I jinxed us.

"HOW LONG DO you think we've been here?" Clove asked, her voice drained.

We'd left the palace behind us more than an hour before. Since night was everlasting, time ceased having meaning.

"I have no idea," Landon said, tightening his arm around my waist as we walked. I was so exhausted I'd taken to resting my head against his shoulder. If sleep while also being awake was possible, I'd totally be able to do it right about now.

"Does anyone remember the other stories in the book?" I asked.

"We haven't done Wonderland yet," Thistle replied. "Or *Beauty and the Beast*. Or whatever the one that features Aladdin is."

"That's disheartening," Landon said. "I was hoping we had one left. Two at the most."

"Something tells me we're going to have to play out more than just the yellow brick road in Oz, too," Thistle said.

"I hadn't thought of that."

My gaze fixed on something to the right of the road, my mind playing tricks on me as I tried to decide what it was. I was so enraptured with the vision I didn't notice that everyone else ceased walking.

"What the ... ?"

"Where did the brick road go?" Marcus asked, confused.

"It just ends," Clove said. "Does that mean we're done with the story?"

"I doubt we're that lucky," Sam said.

"What do you think, Bay?"

I heard them talking, but I was having trouble focusing given the majestic sight taking form in the field next to us. The overlarge moon was bouncing off each glorious green inch of it.

"Bay?" Landon tightened his grip on my hip.

"I think we're done with the brick road," I said, continuing to stare.

"What makes you say that?"

I nodded my chin toward the thousand-foot-tall beanstalk sprouting across the way. "That."

"Oh, no way," Thistle said. "You've got to be kidding me."

"I guess we forgot that story, too."

Landon growled. It was an actual growl. If he was a wolf we'd have to put him down before he ate us. "I just ... there are no words."

"Are we supposed to climb that?" Clove asked, mystified.

"I'm not climbing that," Thistle said, shifting her eyes to me. "Don't even think for a second I'm climbing that! There's nothing you can do to make me climb that. Get it out of your head right now. I'm not going to do it."

"I CAN'T BELIEVE I'm actually doing this," Thistle complained, glancing down at the rapidly diminishing ground as she climbed from one leaf to another. "Tell me again why all of us are doing this instead of just two of us?"

"Because if only two of us did this then you and Marcus would have been the ones who had to do it," I replied, nonplussed.

"How do you figure?"

"I had to be Cinderella."

"I had to kick an ogre in the … knee," Thistle shot back.

"Knock it off," Landon ordered. He was in the lead, and it had been his idea for all of us to climb together. "We all agreed that it was best for the group to go together. No more splitting up."

"Plus, what happens if the next story starts wherever we land up there? Then some of us would be separated at the bottom of the beanstalk and we might never see each other again," I said.

"I can deal with that reasoning," Thistle said. "I still hate climbing."

"It's not so bad," I said. "The leaves are arranged like a spiral staircase."

"An elevator would clearly be better."

I couldn't argue with that. "How much farther?"

"Yeah, are we there yet?" Thistle chimed in.

Landon scowled, his joy at finding me unscathed evaporating with each step. "Can we stop the backseat climbing chatter?"

"Sure," I said.

"No," Thistle said. "Are we there now?"

"Don't make me thump you, Thistle," Landon ordered. "This is hell on all of us."

"Yes, Dad."

"When we get to the top of this beanstalk, I swear … ."

Everyone was quiet for a few minutes. Even though I knew it was probably the wrong move, I broke the silence. "Do you want me to add the beanstalk comment to your book of sayings ideas?"

Landon sighed. "It couldn't hurt."

It took us almost an hour to climb to the top of the beanstalk, and by the time we stepped off the seemingly endless leaves our legs were numb and our feet heavy. We fell to the ground, a spongy expanse of lush grass, panting.

"It's a good thing we all came up here together," Thistle said. "No one would climb back down that beanstalk and then back up again after making that trip. It would've been every couple for themselves."

"See, I was right," Landon said, his hand patting the ground next to me until he found my hand.

"You're always right," I said.

"Don't patronize me."

"I don't have the energy to patronize you," I said. "Do you think we can take a nap here?"

"Sure."

I closed my eyes, weariness overtaking me. "I just need a short nap."

"Me, too," Landon said.

When I mustered the energy to look to my other side I saw Thistle, Clove, Marcus and Sam were already asleep. I'm not sure how I did it, but fear of being separated from Landon during slumber was more overwhelming than the suffocating exhaustion. I shifted over until I could rest my head on his shoulder. Landon wrapped his arm around my back.

"What's wrong, sweetie?"

"I afraid you'll be gone when I wake up. I don't think we're naturally falling asleep. This is part of the next story."

"I won't be gone," Landon said. "I'm too tired to go anywhere. I'll be right here. Trust me."

"I trust you'll try," I said, my eyelids heavy. "The book has control of us. We all know that."

"The book has separated us enough," Landon said. "We'll be okay."

"I hope so." I was barely awake.

"I love you, Bay."

"I love you, too."

We slipped into slumber … and nothing ever felt better.

Beauty is in the eye of the beholder. No, it's true. Looks aren't everything. If a man has a hairy back, though, that's a deal-breaker. Find out what his stance is on waxing his shoulders before you give up the goods. If you can braid a man's back hair, there's a problem.

– *Aunt Tillie's Wonderful World of Stories to Make Little Girls Shut Up*

CHAPTER 15

I woke up to the feeling of grass poking into my cheek.
"Landon?"
I could hear bodies stirring around me.
"Landon?"
Even though sleep was trying to drag me back down I opened my eyes and focused on the spot next to me. It was empty. Landon was gone.

I bolted to a sitting position, scanning the area in case he'd woken up and was looking around to see what fresh new fairy hell awaited us. He was nowhere in sight. "Landon!"

My voice echoed across the open expanse of the castle courtyard. Yes, it seems we'd found a castle. This one was even more majestic than the palace.

"What's going on?" Thistle asked, rubbing her eyes wearily. "Where's Landon?"

"He's gone," I said, pushing myself to my feet and brushing the grass and dirt from my clothes. "I knew this was going to happen." I tried to fight the tears pooling in my eyes.

Thistle wrapped me in a brief hug. "It's just another story."

"Why are we the ones who have been separated three times now?"

"Because Aunt Tillie was really angry at Landon when she cast the curse," Thistle said. "Look at it this way, I'm still the one who had to kiss a frog. It doesn't get much worse than that."

"Thanks, honey," Marcus deadpanned, joining us. "It's going to be okay, Bay. I'm guessing we have to go into the castle and we're going to find Landon there."

"Do you think so?"

"That seems to be the obvious answer."

"Let's get going then. I'm so tired of this."

"We all are," Thistle said. "We all need to remember this feeling."

"Why?"

"Because we're going to need all this anger when we're digging a grave to hide Aunt Tillie's body," Thistle replied.

"You're probably right."

We started moving warily toward the castle. While the castle was tall and proud, the outside was overgrown with dead vines and brambles.

"I'm confused," Clove said as we started climbing the stone stairs that led to the front of the castle. "Why did we all fall asleep?"

"So the curse could separate us again," I said.

"I know I don't remember everything about Aunt Tillie's book, but wasn't there supposed to be a giant at the top of the beanstalk?" Clove asked.

That was a sobering thought. I scanned the open grounds again. There was nothing menacing – other than the bad gardening – to threaten us, though. "I think we would have seen a giant by now if one was here."

"Let's not tempt fate," Thistle said, pushing me forward. "Come on. Landon has to be in here somewhere. Let's find him."

"When we do, I'm tying him to me," I grumbled.

"I'm sure he'll love that."

It took three of us to push the heavy mahogany door open, and the silence that greeted us inside the great foyer was oppressive. The air inside felt stagnant with decay and neglect.

"Well, this is disappointing," Clove said. "Shouldn't a castle be pretty?"

"I think it's pretty," Thistle said. "It needs a good maid, but it's pretty." Her eyes brightened. "Get cleaning, Cinderella."

"Bite me," I muttered.

Five sets of footsteps echoed on the marble floors as we trudged onward. An elegant staircase was built into the wall on our right and a huge set of double doors beckoned at the far end of the hall. We were expecting a giant, but the castle design was meant for normal people.

"What do you think?" Clove asked.

"I think this place is huge, but it's not made for a huge person."

"I mean what direction do you think we should go?"

That was a pretty good question. "I think we should check the whole first floor before going upstairs," I said, considering. "We might as well search in an orderly fashion."

"Are you channeling Landon?" Marcus asked, smiling softly. "He'd be proud."

"Don't talk about him in the past tense," I ordered.

Marcus' face drained of color. "I didn't mean ... ."

"I know you didn't," I said. "Let's find Landon. He somewhere in here ... and he's alone."

"He's going to be fine," Thistle said. "He knows what he's doing."

"I know."

"If it's any consolation, he was worried about you for the same reason when you were whisked away to be Cinderella," Clove added.

"I know," I said. "It's not a consolation, though."

"Come on," Thistle said, taking the lead. "Let's find the Fed. He's probably swearing so much he's making the fairy tale gods tremble."

That was a nice visual.

When we got to the end of the room, Thistle grunted as she pushed the partially-ajar door open and introduced us to a whole new world. Unfortunately, it was a world none of ever wanted to see. The room was ... alive. There was no other way to describe it.

The furniture moved, the curtains danced and the cobwebs in the corner shook in rhythm with music only they could hear. The sound

AMANDA M. LEE

of the door opening stilled the activity, and as a broomstick, candlestick, chair and piano all turned to stare at me I had to swallow the scream that was bubbling up.

"What are they?" It was the candlestick speaking.

"They look like dolls," the piano replied.

"They're pretty ugly dolls," the broomstick said.

"Aren't all dolls ugly?" I wasn't sure who made that comment, but it sounded as though it came from above.

"Um ... ."

"Holy cow," the candlestick said. "The dolls can talk!"

"They're freaking me out. We need to get them out of here before the master comes in and squashes them like bugs."

That sounded ominous. I cleared my throat. "Master?"

"It's talking again!"

I rolled my shoulders, cracking my neck as I fought to contain my temper. "We're not dolls. We're ... people!"

"What's a people?" the broomstick asked. "Does that mean you're an alien?"

"Sure."

"Where is your space ship?"

"It's parked outside," I said. "We lost a member of our ... landing party. If we could find him we'd be out of your hair ... not that you have any hair."

"And out of your master's hair," Clove said. "What? Does anyone else not want to meet their master?"

She wasn't the only one thinking that very thing. "Can you point us toward our missing alien? We'd be very thankful."

"What does he look like?"

"He looks like us," I said. "He has black hair, and he's tall and he's very handsome." I choked up slightly. "He's all alone, and we'd really like to find him."

"There's no one who looks like that here," the candlestick said.

"Are you sure?"

"Sorry."

That was disconcerting.

"Don't worry, Bay. He's here," Marcus said. "We just have to find him."

"We should check upstairs," Clove said. "I'll bet that's where he is."

"Oh, don't go up there," the broomstick warned. "That's where the master is."

"I don't think we have a lot of choice in the matter," I said. "I ... ."

The door at the opposite end of the room opened and the figure standing there was horrific. It was tall and wide, arms too long for its body, and it didn't appear to have a neck. Its face was terrible, overlarge teeth jutting out from its mouth. The brown fur covering its body was long and matted, and when it opened its mouth the only thing that came out was a terrible roar.

"You must be the master," I said, taking an inadvertent step back. "I ... um ... wow."

The creature roared again. It looked like Bigfoot on steroids.

I held up my hand, which shook as I tried to act braver than I felt. "I'm really sorry to come into your home," I said. "We're looking for a friend. We need to find him. We'll be out of your hair as soon as we do. I promise."

The creature shuffled closer, growling as it opened its menacing mouth. I took a step back. "I ... I'm really sorry. We're really sorry."

I glanced over my shoulder, frowning when I saw the empty space behind me – which only moments before had been occupied by Marcus, Thistle, Clove and Sam. "You've got to be kidding me."

The monster roared again, and when I risked a glance back in its direction I realized it was closing the gap between us. "Okay. It's okay. Nice ... thing." I started backing out of the room. "I'm not here to hurt you. I'm assuming you're not here to hurt me. I just ... I need to find someone."

Another roar was all I could take. I fled the room, racing back into the foyer and finding it empty. The open door at the far end of the corridor told me that my supposed family and friends hadn't stopped with abandoning me in a separate room. They'd abandoned me in a strange castle.

The creature screeched behind me again and I increased my pace, bursting from the front of the castle and skidding to a stop on the terrace – where a new horror was waiting.

Thistle, Clove, Marcus and Sam cowered in the far corner, the men working to shield their respective girlfriends, and the hulking figure raising his hands in a menacing fashion on the lawn towered over them.

"Oh, well, I guess we've found the giant," I grumbled.

No one answered except for the monster closing the distance on me from behind. Things officially just got worse. How was that even possible?

THE GIANT SCREAMED, ramming his hands down on the ground with enough force to shake the courtyard – and the castle behind us. Apparently in Aunt Tillie's head a giant has more in common with the Hulk than anything else.

"Well, great," I said. "This is just awesome. We have a giant cutting us off from escape in that direction and the hairy beast is coming after me from in there. Thanks for having my back in there, by the way. I just loved turning around and finding myself alone ... again."

"We thought you were right behind us," Marcus said, covering Thistle's head.

"Well, I wasn't."

"Do you really think this is the time to argue about this?" Marcus asked, infuriated. "Get over here."

He was panicked. He was doing his best to hold it together, but without Landon here to tell everyone what to do we were scattered. We lacked leadership. We were ... a mess. Where was he?

Instead of doing as Marcus instructed I turned to face the giant and descended the stairs.

"Bay! What are you doing?" Marcus screamed.

I ignored him and kept moving forward. The giant stilled when he saw me, a meaty fist raised high above his head. I was ... done. I couldn't take another second of this.

"I don't know if you're watching this, Aunt Tillie," I said, my eyes clouding with angry tears. "Enough is enough, though. We want to go home. We need to go home. You've taught us our lessons. Please. Give me back Landon and ... end this. I believe you can hear me.

"That's what you told me, right?" I continued. "At the Cinderella house you told me that everything depended on what we believe. I believe we should be done here. So ... I'm done."

For one brief, shining moment I thought I'd won. The giant cocked its head to the side, its eyes softening. Then the world tilted as the giant roared and aimed its descending fist at me.

My body flew to the side as something barreled into me from behind. Another roaring voice entered the fray, only this one belonged to the hairy castle beast. After tossing me out of the way, the growling monster caught the giant's descending fist and deflected it, whimpering from the force of the blow.

The monster matched the giant angry howl for angry howl. I rolled over on my side so I could glance back at the castle. Marcus was on his feet staring at me, worry marring his handsome face as he debated running after me or staying to protect Thistle and Clove. He was caught. He knew it, and I knew it, too.

"Stay there," I yelled. "Don't come out here."

Marcus didn't look convinced. "Bay! Come back here. I can't just leave you. I made a promise to Landon."

What promise? "So did I," I said. "I won't leave this place without him."

"That's not what I'm saying," Marcus said. "Come back here! We'll figure it out. Let them fight. It's what they want to do."

I shook my head, turning back to the battle raging in front of me. The giant was stronger, but the beast was determined. I had no idea why it pushed me out of the way and sacrificed itself in the battle. It was almost as if ... .

"Oh, crap." I pushed myself to my feet, realization dawning as I searched for a weapon. There wasn't much to choose from. The only thing that was even remotely an option was a large rock half buried in the ground.

I dug my fingers into the hard dirt, grimacing at the pain as I clawed at the rock. It took everything I had to dislodge it, and when I had it in my hand I turned back to the giant.

The beast was on the ground, struggling to regain its footing as it continued to put its battered body between me and the giant. I didn't take time to think about what I was doing. I didn't care whether it was smart. I didn't care whether it would work. It was the only thing I could do, so I did it.

I launched the rock at the giant's head as hard as I could. He was readying himself for another blow against the beast, but when the rock hit him in the head he shifted his attention to me.

The beast howled, enraged, but the giant ignored it. I was on the menu now.

I didn't take a step back, and I didn't try to protect myself. Instead, I spoke the words I knew would end the story. I remembered this one from Aunt Tillie's book. "Sometimes you have to fight, even though you know you're going to lose," I yelled, clenching my hands into fists at my side. "I can't win, but I won't stop fighting!"

The giant's face blanked at the words and then, like magic, it started dissolving. Within seconds, the only thing that remained was the beast ... and my tears.

The beast breathed heavily, and it listed to one side and dropped to a knee, giving in to fatigue now that the danger was gone. I closed the distance between us, the lyrics of an old song playing through my head.

When I got close to the beast I leaned down, searching the clear eyes that stared back at me. "You promised we wouldn't be separated again," I said, grabbing either side of its face. "I love you!"

I closed my eyes and leaned forward, pressing my lips against the beast's. I could hear the zip of magic, and when I opened my eyes Landon stared at me in astonishment.

"How did you know?"

"No one else would be willing to die for me," I said.

"I think you're wrong on that front," Landon said, reaching for me. "I can't believe you did that."

"Sometimes you have to fight for the person you love," I said, bursting into tears.

"You do indeed," Landon said, pulling me close as we sank to the ground. "Oh, cripes, you scared me half to death. Don't cry. If you don't stop crying, I'm going to cry. Oh, well, crap. I guess we'll both cry."

If someone tries to distract you by making you look in a specific direction, make sure you look the other way. The one thing they're trying to hide from you is usually the one thing you need to find. That's only true if I'm not the one trying to hide something from you, though. If I tell you to knock it off, I mean it.

– Aunt Tillie's Wonderful World of Stories to Make Little Girls Shut Up

CHAPTER 16

*L*andon and I remained wrapped around one another for at least five minutes. We didn't glance up until someone cleared a throat behind us.

"Now is not a good time," Landon growled, tightening his arm around my shoulder. "I can't tell you how ticked off I am at you guys right now."

"What did we do?" Thistle protested.

Landon stiffened. "Well, for starters, you bolted and left Bay to fend for herself. Way to be loyal."

"Hey, you were terrifying," Thistle said.

"We thought she was right behind us," Marcus offered sincerely. "I didn't realize she wasn't until we were already on the terrace … and by then we had another problem."

"Whatever," Landon grumbled. "You still left her in there. What if she'd been hurt?"

"Were you going to hurt her?" Thistle asked.

"You didn't know it was me," Landon said. "By the way, in my head I was talking regularly but it kept coming out in growls. I wasn't trying to frighten you."

"I know," I said, pulling my face away to study him. "Are you hurt?"

"I'm fine. Are you hurt?"

"I was so worried about you," I said. "When I woke up ... you were gone."

"I'm so sorry," Landon said, cupping my chin. "I shouldn't have promised I would be there when we woke up. This world doesn't give us the luxury of keeping promises."

"It's not as if I thought you walked away on purpose," I said.

Landon arched an eyebrow.

"I didn't," I said. "Not this time. It didn't even enter my head."

"That's good, Bay," Landon said. "No one is leaving. Not again."

I snorted. "Don't say that just yet," I said. "We're trapped in a fairy tale world. We still don't have control."

"I know," Landon said. "I wasn't talking about here, though."

I rested my forehead against his briefly. "I know."

Landon pressed me to his chest as he rolled us to a different position. He climbed to his feet and pulled me along with him, never letting go of me. When we were standing, the look he shot Marcus was chilling. "I'm not thrilled with you right now."

"What did you expect me to do?" Marcus asked. "She ran right into danger. She wasn't the only one here."

"I know that," Landon said. "I also know that Thistle is your first priority. You still left her."

"I ... ." Marcus' cheeks colored with shame. "I'm sorry. Clove ran, and Sam ran after her. Then Thistle took off and ... instinct took over. I swear I thought Bay was right behind us. I wouldn't have abandoned her."

"I know," Landon said, running his hand over the back of my head. "I heard you during the fight."

"I ... I'm sorry."

"Don't worry about it," Landon said, coldly. "We're all fine. We're all getting out of here."

"Landon, I really am sorry," Marcus said.

"I told you not to worry about it," Landon said. "We're all exhausted. We're all ... frustrated. I want out of here."

"Where do we go next?" Thistle asked, linking her fingers with

Marcus' as she rested her head against his shoulder in a sign of solidarity.

"The castle," Landon said.

"How do you know that?" I asked.

"It's a feeling. I think the castle is our end location. We have to figure out how many fairy tales we're talking about here."

"Let's go," I said, slipping my arm around his waist. "Are you sure you're not hurt?"

"The second I changed back all of my aches and pains went away," Landon said, kissing my forehead. "Well … except one. You're here, though. You're fixing that one."

I wanted to cry again. "Landon … ."

"No, Bay, not now," he said. "We're okay. Everyone is okay. Let's finish this. I want to go home."

"All right," I said. "Let's do it."

"We'll be right behind you," Marcus said.

Landon ignored the proffered promise.

"**WHAT** HAPPENED TO THE TALKING CANDLESTICK?"

I shrugged, unsure. The busy room from before was different now. The candlestick was gone. The broomstick, devoid of life, leaned against the wall. The cobwebs and decay had been replaced with a bright and shiny cleaning. It was the same castle, yet everything was different.

"What do you think?" Landon asked.

"I don't know," I said. "We still have a few stories to go through. This doesn't jump out as anything I recognize."

"Maybe we're done," Clove suggested. "Maybe we only have to find a way out."

"No," I said, shaking my head. "There's no way we're getting out of here without a nod to Wonderland and Oz," I said. "Those were Aunt Tillie's favorites. There's a reason we haven't hit them yet. They're going to be the big finale."

"How do you know that?" Thistle asked.

"It's Aunt Tillie. She's not going to let us out of here without forcing us to go through those stories."

"Is that how you knew how to beat the giant?" Clove asked. "I couldn't believe you did that, and yet as you were saying the words I realized I remembered them."

"I'm not sure how I remembered to beat the giant," I said. "I only know that I realized the beast was Landon before I decided to fight the giant. Once I realized it was him, I didn't have a choice."

"You had another choice," Landon said.

"No, I didn't."

Landon's face softened. "You're my brave girl." He pulled me in for a brief hug. "If this was the real world, though, I'd be yelling at you for risking yourself."

"I know."

"Since this is a fairy tale world, I'm going to give you a pass."

"Thanks."

"Are you saying what you think I want to hear because you don't want to argue?" Landon asked.

I smiled. "You're very handsome."

Landon grinned. "That's what I thought." He leaned over and gave me a soft kiss. "I desperately need to get out of this place. Not only do I need breakfast, I need to make sure we have a day in bed to recuperate."

"What about punishing Aunt Tillie?"

"We'll do that first," Landon said, winking.

"Good to know."

The room lapsed into silence, everyone searching for clues to our next destination. When a hint of movement caught my attention on the far wall I shifted my head and focused on the shadow. It looked like the plant in front of the window and yet … there was more to it.

I narrowed my eyes and focused, sucking in a breath when the shadow moved on its own accord. I tilted my head to the side, studying the shadow. I risked a glance over my shoulder, but nothing moved behind me. When I glanced back at the wall, the shadow had moved away from the plant and now stood alone. It was also in the shape of a person.

"Uh, guys ... ."

"What's up, sweetie?" Landon asked, moving to my side.

I pointed at the shadow, which refused to move.

"What am I looking at?" Landon asked, confused.

"The shadow is moving."

Landon focused on it. "No, it's not."

"It was."

Landon shifted so he could look over his shoulder, and the second he did the shadow waved at me. It froze again when Landon turned back. "There's nothing back there moving."

"No," I agreed. "The second you turned your head, though, it waved at me."

"It did?"

"Yup."

"Is Bay seeing things now?" Thistle asked, smirking.

"No one is talking to you," Landon snapped.

He was angry. It practically rolled off of him. He was trying to control himself, at least delay an argument, but I was the only one he wasn't angry with right now. That was a nice change of pace.

The shadow moved again. "There!"

"I saw it," Thistle said, giving Landon a wide berth as she moved around him and settled on my other side. We exchanged an eyebrow lift and then focused back on the shadow. It was playing a game, jumping from one shadow to the next and then poking its head out to wave at us.

"What do we think this means?" Sam asked.

"It's Peter Pan," I said.

"Does that mean we're going to Neverland?" Sam looked excited at the prospect. "Sorry, I just loved that story when I was a kid."

"It always reminded me of *Lord of the Flies*," Thistle replied drily.

"What?" Sam was incensed. "How can you say that?"

"A bunch of boys on an island with nothing to do but cause trouble? It's total anarchy."

"You obviously didn't get the point of the story," Sam said.

"She has a point," I said. "I think Peter Pan, just like *Lord of the Flies*, is a cautionary tale of what happens to men if they don't have women in their lives to temper the crazy."

Landon barked out a hoarse laugh. "That's kind of funny."

"It's not true, though," Sam protested. "Peter Pan is a great role model!"

"He wears tights and tempts kids out of their bedrooms at night so they can terrify their parents into thinking someone kidnapped them," Thistle countered. "Then they fly to a land where no one wants to grow up and you're either a pirate who doesn't care about killing kids or a kid who has nothing better to do than terrorize adults. That doesn't sound healthy to me."

I could tell Landon was fighting the urge to smile, his anger with Thistle and especially Marcus still at the forefront of his mind, but he was having a good time watching Thistle crush Sam's childhood dreams.

The shadow dove to the dark spot on the far wall, and this time when it poked out it beckoned to us.

"I think it wants us to follow it," Clove said. "Do you think we should?"

"I think we're going to set these last stories up and knock them down," I said, resolved. "This is the next one. Let's get to it."

Landon grabbed my hand as I started to move. "Don't you even think about stepping away from me," he said. "We're doing this together."

"Of course we are," I said. "I couldn't do it without you."

"I feel like puking," Thistle said.

"Don't push me, Thistle," Landon warned.

"No one push anyone," I said. "We're close here, people. We only have to stick together for a little bit longer. Let's not fall apart now."

"Fine," Landon said through his clenched jaw. "When this is over with, though, I want a whole day of just you and me. I don't want to see a single member of your family. I'm talking a full twenty-four hours."

"We'll go to a hotel," I promised.

"You bet we're going to a hotel," Landon said. "You're going to pay, too."

"Okay."

"We're getting nothing but room service," Landon said, pulling me as he started to follow the shadow. "We're getting breakfast in bed, lunch in bed and dinner in bed."

"That sounds fun," Clove said. "Maybe we'll go with you."

Sam shot her a quelling look.

"Maybe not," Clove said quickly. "Sorry."

"I'm not joking, Bay," Landon said. "We need a break from all this … togetherness."

"Maybe you should go to the hotel alone," I suggested. "You don't look too happy with me right now."

"You're the only thing making me happy right now. Never doubt that."

"OKAY, does anyone think this is the weirdest setting yet?" Thistle leaned over and rested her hand against the giant toadstool, snatching it away after a few seconds of contact. "That feels funny."

"It's a giant mushroom," Landon said. "What did you expect it to feel like?"

"I don't know," Thistle said, ignoring his sarcasm. "It looks like it's made out of plastic. I thought it would feel smooth."

"It smells," Clove said.

"It's a mushroom," Landon said.

"I wish we had our phones," Thistle said. "I would love a cool photo on top of the toadstool."

"It's a giant mushroom!" Landon was beside himself.

After following the shadow through the labyrinth of hallways and out a side door of the castle, we'd spent the last ten minutes studying the peculiar setting. The shadow disappeared, which meant whatever was supposed to happen would occur in this area. I was almost sure of it.

"Which story is this?" Landon asked.

"I'm not sure yet."

"Why is nothing happening?"

"I don't know."

"What do you know?"

"I know you're upset," I said, setting my hand on his forearm. "I'm sorry. I ... ."

"No, I'm sorry," Landon said, shaking his head. "This isn't your fault. I did this."

"How do you figure that?"

"I'm the one who threatened her," Landon said, rubbing his forehead. "I'm the one who promised to confiscate her wine. She probably would have ignored us if I hadn't been so ... harsh."

"You shouldn't blame yourself for doing your job," I said. "Aunt Tillie is the one at fault here, not you."

"She's right," Thistle said. "Aunt Tillie knew what she was doing was wrong. That's why she tried to hide it. If she thought she was in the right she would have told everyone what she was doing. She likes to brag."

"I'm sorry I'm being so cranky," Landon said. "This situation is ... out of our control. I don't like Bay being in danger. I don't like any of us being in danger. It feels as though this thing is never going to end."

"It's going to end," I said. "I think we have only two left."

"Which two?"

"Wonderland and Oz."

"Which one is this?" Landon asked.

"I ... ." I jumped back when a huge rabbit barreled between us, the furry beast tripping over the toadstool and hitting the ground hard on the other side.

"Who put that there?" the rabbit asked, flummoxed. "Has someone been rearranging furniture?"

Thistle's face split with a wide grin. "This is the best one!"

Landon scowled. "Wonderland?"

I nodded. "This was always Thistle's favorite story."

"I have to get moving," the rabbit said. "I'm running behind. This is not good. This is so not good." The rabbit glanced at us, irritated. "Put that toadstool back where you found it. It doesn't belong there."

We all watched, slack jawed, as the rabbit got back to its feet and hurried around the corner of the house.

"Follow that rabbit," Thistle instructed, breaking into a run. "Hurry! I don't want to miss this one!"

"Well, at least someone is excited," Landon said, grabbing my hand. "If you're right, once we get through this one there's only one left."

"I think I'm right."

"I have faith in you," Landon said. "Let's go. If we don't keep an eye on Thistle she's going to molest that rabbit. Did you see the look on her face when she saw it?"

"It is kind of cool," I said, following Landon. "Don't tell me you don't think it's cool."

"I'm beyond anything being cool in this world," he said. "The only thing I'm going to find cool in the foreseeable future is a bath, a bed and a plateful of bacon."

"I'll make sure you get all three of them," I said.

"We're going to get all three of them together," Landon said. "No one is in this alone, especially you and me."

Tea doesn't constitute a party – unless there's bourbon in the cup, too. Now, that's a party. You can't go to those types of parties yet. Forget I told you that.

– Aunt Tillie's Wonderful World of Stories to Make Little Girls Shut Up

CHAPTER 17

By the time we rounded the corner of the castle, Thistle had a significant lead on us. Marcus broke into a run to catch up with her, while Landon and I slowed our approach to give ourselves time to study the outrageous tableau.

"What is that?" Sam asked, confused.

I smiled. "It's a tea party."

"There are a lot of animals standing on two feet and kind of ... hanging out," Sam said.

"It's Wonderland," I said. "Nothing is normal."

"What's the lesson in this one?" Landon asked.

I racked my brain, trying to prod a memory forward. "All I remember about this one is that Aunt Tillie doesn't believe that a tea party is a real party unless people are slipping bourbon into the tea cups."

Landon snorted. "That sounds about right. She's got her fingerprints all over this world."

"What should we do?" Clove asked, worried. "We're never going to be able to tear Thistle away from this one."

"It's Aunt Tillie's world," I reminded her. "Nothing is as it seems, and nothing is safe. This might look like a tea party, but there's a lot more going on in Wonderland besides tea."

"That's true," Clove said. "What do you want to do?"

"We have to join the party," I said. "That's where this is all going to begin."

"I'm worried about where it's going to end," Clove said.

She wasn't the only one.

I led Landon to one of the tables, pulling out a chair and directing him to sit while I kept an eye on Thistle. She was having a great time chatting up a turtle. Marcus was beside her, but his eyes were busy scanning for hidden threats.

After a few seconds I realized Landon wasn't sitting. Instead he stood next to me, an unreadable expression on his face.

"What?" I asked.

"You just pulled my chair out," Landon said.

"So?"

"I'm still the prince," he said, pushing my hand away. "I pull your chair out."

"Oh, you're so macho," I grumbled.

"If that's how you want to think about me, that's fine." Landon pulled my chair out and gestured to it. "Milady."

I rolled my eyes but took the seat. This wasn't worth arguing about. Landon settled next to me, unfolding the cloth napkin and looking around. "What do you think we're waiting for?"

"I'm not sure yet," I said. "There are a lot of different parts in that book, and there are technically two books. Aunt Tillie could have picked any part of them to incorporate into her book.

"I remember Thistle was always correcting Aunt Tillie when she told us Wonderland stories," I continued. "Thistle was like a film critic who couldn't stand when the director broke from the source material. It totally ticked her off."

"Thistle doesn't strike me as a fairy tale kid," Landon said, reaching for the pot of tea. "Do you think it's safe to drink this?"

I nodded, watching as he poured my cup and then his own. "What do you mean?"

"I always associate fairy tales with girly girls," he said.

"Do you associate fairy tales with me?"

"Are you asking whether I think of you as a girly girl?"

"I ... don't know," I said. "I don't know what answer would freak me out more."

"Sometimes I try to picture you as a kid," Landon said. "All I see is long, blonde hair and pigtails. I see you running in the woods, and I see you wrestling around with Thistle. I don't see dresses ... or dolls ... or tiaras."

"That's probably good," I said. "I never liked any of those things."

"That's what I figured," Landon said, sipping his tea. "Thistle wasn't like that either, was she?"

"No."

"What about Clove?"

I looked to the next table, smiling when I saw Clove and Sam talking with a giant squirrel. "Clove liked dolls and dresses," I said. "At a certain point she tried to pretend she didn't, because she wanted to be like Thistle and me."

"That sounds like her."

"I don't think it was fair to her, though," I said. "I often wonder whether Clove would have been better off with two cousins who weren't so ... overbearing."

"I don't think of you as overbearing," Landon said. "Don't get me wrong, you have your moments. Given how overbearing some of the other women in your life are – and yes I'm referring to Thistle and Aunt Tillie – you're much mellower than you have any business being."

"I don't know," I shrugged. "It's hard to look back at your childhood without regret."

"I don't think you should regret anything," Landon said. "I think you turned out pretty terrific."

"You do?"

"I don't know any other woman who would take on a giant and kiss a hairy monster on faith alone."

"You're right," I said. "I am pretty great!"

Landon's grin was adorable. "You are." He leaned forward and rubbed his nose against mine briefly. "I'm so ready to get us out of here."

"You and me both."

"Oh, Craig, look who it is."

I froze when I heard the voice, turning my head from Landon and focusing on the three bears standing at the other side of the table. "Oh ... hey."

"I see you found a friend," Sheila said, hoisting her impressive girth onto one of the metal bistro chairs. "We were worried about you after you left."

"I wasn't worried," Sebastian said. "I was hoping something ate you."

Landon made a face. "Do you want to introduce me to your friends?"

"Sure," I said. "This is Craig, Sheila and Sebastian. They're the bears I was telling you about. This is Landon. He's my boyfriend."

"Oh, that's nice," Craig said, sitting next to his wife. "Did you know that your girlfriend climbed into our beds last night?"

"I heard," Landon said, leaning back in his chair and slinging an arm around my shoulders. "She's always been adventurous."

"Is that code for something?" Sebastian asked.

"Not really."

"Your girlfriend jumped in strangers' beds," Sebastian said. "That doesn't sound like a very good girlfriend."

"We've moved on from it," Landon said, changing tactics. "We had a big fight but now we're over it. She was only doing it to make me jealous."

"I had to sleep on the couch because of her," Sebastian complained.

"Let it go, son," Craig said. "It's in the past."

"I didn't know you were invited to this party," I said. "Do you know who's hosting it?"

"Don't you?" Sheila asked.

"I'm guessing it's the Mad Hatter," I said. "Am I right?"

Sheila tilted her head to the side and gave what passed for a smile. "Not exactly."

I didn't like her tone. "I have to ask you guys something," I said, lifting my hand and rubbing Landon's fingers as they idly moved across my shoulder. "Do you know you're in a book?"

"Of course we know we're in a book," Sheila said. "We're not stupid."

"Do we know we're in a book," Craig chortled. "For a human, you're cute."

"Do you know who wrote the book?"

"The most wonderful scribe in the land," Sebastian said.

"And who is that?"

"The great and powerful Tillie," Sebastian replied, solemn.

"I knew it," I said, pumping my first. "I told you Wonderland and Oz were the last ones."

"You're very wise, sweetie," Landon said, topping off my cup of tea.

"Have you ever met the great and powerful Tillie?" I asked.

"No," Sheila said. "They say if you look upon her in the flesh you'll never be seen again."

That sounded like her. It really did. "Is Tillie hosting this tea party?" Hey, I can hope.

"Of course not," Craig said. "The great and powerful Tillie doesn't drink tea unless it's laced with bourbon. Plus, she's very busy. She runs the entire land."

"From where?"

"Here."

I glanced around. "The castle?"

Sheila nodded. "This is her home."

"I thought this was the beast's home," I said.

"What beast?"

Hmm. It seems some tales had problems crossing over. "How long as Tillie been in charge of this land?"

"Since it was created," Craig said.

"And when was that?"

"When the world started," Craig said.

"But ... when?"

"Back when she started it," Craig said, flustered.

"What are you trying to do here?" Landon asked, keeping his voice low. "Are you trying to agitate the bears?"

"No," I said. "I'm trying to find out whether they have a sense of time."

"Why?"

"Because they're self-aware," I said. "They're not real, but in a way they're self-aware. The thought of them ... winking out of existence ... makes me a little sad."

"Bay ... ."

"It's okay," I said. "I'm not an idiot. I know I can't change this. I'm trying to get a feeling for what's going on."

"Okay," Landon said, "but I don't want you to have a broken heart when we finally get out of here. That's going to be one of the happiest moments of my life. I don't want you feeling sad about anything."

I glanced at him, curious. "What are the other happiest times of your life?"

"Are you fishing for a compliment?"

"No," I said. "I honestly want to know."

"Well, the first Christmas I remember I got a new bike," he said. "I remember going down the stairs and seeing it and thinking that nothing could ever be better than that. Then the first time I ... you know ... that was pretty exciting."

I made a face.

"Not nearly as exciting as you, sweetie," he teased.

"You're still charming," I said.

"I try."

"What else?" I prodded.

"The day I graduated from high school. The day I was recruited into the bureau. The day I met you."

"You hated me the day we met," I said. "You thought I was mouthy and in your way."

"That's not true," Landon said. "I liked you from the moment I saw you."

"You're making that up."

"I'm not," Landon said. "That was truly one of the greatest moments in my life. Do you want to know what the single greatest moment of my life was, though?"

I waited.

"The night you told me you loved me."

My cheeks colored, and I lowered my gaze. "Oh."

"What about you?" Landon asked. "What's your greatest moment?"

"Right now," I said, averting my gaze.

Landon exhaled heavily. "We seriously need to get out of here," he said. "There are so many things I'd rather be doing right now, and not one of them involves having tea with bears. No offense."

"None taken," Sheila said. "I love seeing young people in love. I really hope you survive the sacrifice."

"Thank you for saying that," I said, warmth washing over me. "I … wait, what did you say?"

"I hope you survive the sacrifice," Sheila repeated. "We hear it's going to be a real bloodbath this year."

"That's why we came," Sebastian said. "We love a good blood sacrifice."

"What do you mean?" I asked. "Who is going to sacrifice who?"

"The queen, of course," Craig said. "It's her annual tea. She always sacrifices the humans when she hosts a tea."

Crap. Here was the twist on Wonderland. I gripped Landon's hand. "We need to get out of here," I said. "I have a bad feeling about this."

"I'm right there with you," Landon said, jumping to his feet. "We need to bypass this one right now and get into the castle. That's where we're going to find the last story. I think we're done with this one."

I scanned the crowd. "Do you see anyone else?"

"I got distracted," Landon said. "I stopped watching them."

I jerked my head back and forth, studying the assembled animals. "Do you notice we're the only humans left?"

"I'm guessing that's a bad sign," Landon said.

"I'm guessing that's the worst sign ever," I said. "We have to move."

I reached for his hand, but when I met air I swiveled quickly, panicking.

The rabbit was back, and he had a knife at Landon's throat. "Did you move that toadstool back? I didn't think so. I can't stand furniture movers."

"Let him go," I ordered.

"I can't do that," the rabbit said. "The pleasure of your company is requested for a very special meeting with the queen."

I ran my tongue over my teeth, conflicted. Had Clove, Thistle, Marcus and Sam already been taken? Was I the only one left standing? Could I fight everyone on my own? I gave in. "Take me to your queen."

"Run, Bay," Landon ordered. "Don't do this."

"You said it yourself," I said. "We're in this together."

"But ... ."

I shook my head. "We're in this together."

The rabbit smiled, unleashing a row of razor-sharp teeth. "Follow me."

"I'll be right behind you."

THE RABBIT never released Landon as he led us through a thick tangle of trees. In the grand scheme of things, the trek was short. It felt longer because my mind was so busy. How were we going to get out of this one?

Once the trees thinned we found ourselves in a huge clearing. A large and garish throne, all yellow gold and red velvet, sat empty in the middle of the space, a handful of armored guards standing at either side.

Sam and Clove were on their knees on one side of the throne, two guards watching over them. Thistle and Marcus were in the same position on the other side. I met Thistle's worried gaze from across the expanse. We were in trouble now.

"Where's the queen?" I asked.

"She doesn't show herself until all the sacrifices are in place," the rabbit said. "You two are the last ones."

"Awesome," I said. "I can't wait to meet her. I've heard a lot about her."

"I'm sure you have," the rabbit said. "Move up to the spot between the other two couples and kneel."

"Don't you dare kneel, Bay," Landon said.

The rabbit pulled the knife closer to Landon's throat. "Don't make me hurt him."

My gaze bounced between them for a moment. "I'll kneel," I said. "Just ... don't hurt him."

Landon scowled, watching me move to the designated spot. I dropped to my knees. By the time Landon was deposited next to me, two guards were already in place to make sure we didn't make a break for it.

"You should have run," Landon said.

"I'm not leaving you."

"You're not going to think that's such a good idea if we die here," he said.

"We're not going to die here."

"How can you be sure?"

"I have faith."

"That's good," Landon said. "Because here comes the queen."

I lifted my head, frowning as the imposing figure cut a swath through the armored guards and headed for her throne. Her dress was wider than it was tall, and the red was so bright and tacky it hurt my eyes to gaze upon it. It was the face at the top of the dress that threw me, though.

"You've got to be kidding me," I said, my heart rolling.

The woman started to speak. "I am the Queen of Hearts. You are here to serve as my sacrifices."

"Oh, come on," I said. "I can't be killed by my own mother! This is ... I'm going to kill Aunt Tillie!"

Sometimes the person who you think is your enemy is actually your friend. Sometimes your enemy is your enemy, though. When in doubt, go ahead and curse with impunity. You can always sort out the mess later.

– *Aunt Tillie's Wonderful World of Stories to Make Little Girls Shut Up*

CHAPTER 18

"Why is your mother the Queen of Hearts?" Thistle asked, horrified. "I ... she would kill Aunt Tillie if she saw that dress. She looks as though she has the hips of a horse. No, it's more like the hips of four horses."

I had a feeling I knew exactly why Mom was taking on one of the most bloodthirsty children's tale roles of all time. "Who was Aunt Tillie furious with before we left the inn last night? Is it still last night? It's as if we're stuck in a nightmare that refuses to quit. I have no concept of time."

"She was angry with Landon," Thistle said. "He threatened to confiscate her wine."

"How did he even know about it, though? Who told on her?"

"Oh," Thistle said, realization dawning. "Right now she sees your mother as the one who betrayed her. She expected Landon to be the bad guy because he's with the fuzz. She didn't expect it from our mothers. Is anyone else afraid to find out what she did to our mothers?"

"I'm sure it was just as creative as this," I said.

"Do you think she put them into a book, too?"

"If she did, I'm betting it was a terrible book," I said.

"Like *Dracula*?"

"She probably put them in that new *The Walking Dead* graphic novel collection she bought last week," Clove said. "She's been obsessed with zombies lately."

Well, that was an interesting thought. Maybe Mom and my aunts had it worse than us after all.

"I would rather be in a zombie book," Landon said. "At least then I'd probably have a gun. I really feel like shooting someone right now."

"Mom?"

Landon shrugged, reticent. "Maybe. Don't ever tell her I said that."

"Your secret is safe with me."

"Are you done with your little … conversation?" Mom asked, her voice shrill as she glared at us. I felt as though I was eight years old again and we'd just gotten caught plotting how to steal fresh cookies from the kitchen counter. "We have a bit of a schedule to stick to here."

"A schedule?"

"I have a long speech to make," Mom said. "I like to talk and talk and talk – even when no one wants to listen. That's the way I am. Then I have to behead you. After that, I have a tea to get to."

"Does anyone else find it funny that even while trapped in a book Aunt Winnie is working from a schedule?" Clove asked.

"She's a control freak," Thistle said. "They're all control freaks. I like how she's describing herself just as Aunt Tillie would, though."

"You guys are control freaks, too," Sam said. "Don't kid yourselves."

"Hey!" Clove shot him a look. "I am not a control freak."

"You spent two hours rearranging the shelves in Hypnotic back to the way they were before Thistle dusted the other day," Sam said, nonplussed. "Everything was still on the same shelf – only slightly off – and you were dancing like you had ants in your pants waiting for Thistle to leave the store so you could fix everything just the way you like it."

"I knew it!" Thistle seethed, shifting so she could glare at Clove. "I told you those shelves looked different when I came back from the stables and you said I was imagining things. You're a freak."

"Those shelves are immaculate now," Clove sniffed. "I don't know what you're complaining about."

"They were immaculate when I got done with them," Thistle said.

"Not really."

"When we get out of here, you're dead to me," Thistle said.

"What else is new?"

"I agree that Clove is a control freak like our mothers," Thistle said, scorching her with a look. "I'm not a control freak, though."

"You're the worst one," Landon said, "only you feel the need to control people, not things."

"Whatever," Thistle grumbled. "You're the bossy one."

"I'm not bossy," Landon shot back. "I'm ... ." He looked to me for help.

"Handsome," I supplied.

"You're supposed to say I'm not bossy," Landon said.

"Oh, I didn't know you wanted me to lie," I said.

"If I had a list, you'd be at the top of it right now," Landon said.

I couldn't help but smile. "I'd be happy to be at the top of your list."

"See, now you're cute again." Landon leaned over and kissed me.

"What is going on here?" Mom's voice was unnaturally shrill. "You're about to be sacrificed and you're ... having a good time?"

Landon dissolved into hearty guffaws as he shifted from his knees to his rear end and sat on the grass. He laughed so hard his shoulders shook.

"Landon has officially lost it," Thistle said. "He's been pushed too far. His mind has shattered."

"Are you all right?" I asked, worried. He did look a little deranged.

"This has been one of the worst nights of my life," he said, running his hand through his disheveled hair. "I've been hit on by a foul-mouthed mermaid. I've had to shove an unconscious witch into an oven. I've lost my girlfriend and had to steal her back from some ponce in tights who stole her shoe and screamed like a woman.

"I've been turned into a beast and had to fight a giant," he continued. "I seriously thought my heart was going to rip in two when Bay put herself in danger ... but then she was the one who saved me. Then

I had tea with some bears and now my girlfriend's mother is going to behead us."

"Yup, he's lost it," Clove said.

"This has also been one of the … best nights of my life," Landon said, rubbing the back of his neck wearily.

I raised my eyebrows. "It has?"

"I saw you dressed like a princess and I got to carry you around," Landon said. "I got to watch Thistle stab a wolf while wearing a red cloak. You figured out I was a monster and still wanted to kiss me. We've gotten to talk and hang out and spend time together.

"Sure, climbing the beanstalk was terrible and I'm really not looking forward to being beheaded … but I wouldn't trade the time I've spent with you tonight for anything," he said.

"I think I might cry," I said.

"Me, too," Clove said, putting her hand to her heart. She used her free hand to punch Sam in the arm. "How come you never say romantic things like that to me?"

"I think I'm going to puke," Thistle said. "I can't believe that you're making some grand pronouncement now. Can't you help us get out of this situation and then get all schmaltzy?"

"You and I are cut from the same cloth," Mom said, pointing at Thistle. "That was utterly ridiculous."

"I told you that you were becoming a villain," I said when Thistle balked.

"I am not a villain," Thistle said, placing her hands on her hips and shaking her head angrily. "Just because you like things the way you like them does not make you a villain. Am I mean? Yes. I don't always mean to be. I can't control what comes out of my mouth sometimes."

"That's a family trait," Marcus said. "I wouldn't worry about it."

"That's not the point," Thistle said.

"What is the point?" I asked.

"The point is I'm not a villain," Thistle said. "I'm a … complicated princess."

"Oh, you're definitely a princess," Marcus said, running his hand over her short-cropped hair and pulling her over so he could kiss her forehead. "You're the best princess ever."

"Oh, now I'm jealous of Thistle and Marcus," Clove complained.

"I always treat you like a princess," Sam said. "I resent you going all … pouty … when these two spout platitudes because I'm always making romantic pronouncements. I read you poetry the other night and then watched *The Notebook* with you. I never complained once. I've always been your prince."

Clove sighed. "You have. I'm sorry."

"I can't believe this," Mom shrieked. "You're supposed to be focusing on me! I'm the center of attention here! I'm the queen!"

"Do you think that's how Aunt Tillie really sees your mom?" Thistle asked. "Do you think she sees her as the despot in our little fiefdom and she's always bossing her around?"

"I think Aunt Tillie has a warped sense of the world," I said. "I think this is exactly how she sees Mom, though."

"How do you think she sees my mom?" Thistle asked.

"She's the court jester," Landon said, grinning.

Thistle made a face, but it didn't last long. "I can see that."

"Now that you've all played kissy face and … whatever it is you're doing … can we please get back to the issue at hand?" Mom demanded. "I have a schedule!"

"Here's my schedule," I said, pushing myself from the ground and dusting off the seat of my pants. "We're done. We don't want to play this game. We're not going to be beheaded. We're not going to sit here and listen to you complain and make a speech. We're done!"

I extended my hand to help Landon up. Thistle, Clove, Sam and Marcus rose to their feet, too.

"We're going to go into the castle now," I said. "We're going to find the great and powerful Tillie and we're going to go home."

"The great and powerful Tillie?" Thistle asked.

"Oh, I forgot you weren't there to hear that part," I said. "Yeah, the bears told us. She lives in the castle."

"Well, that figures," Thistle said. "She's always had an inflated sense of ego."

"I'm not sure that's true in this case," I said. "She did create this world, after all."

"I guess," Thistle conceded, "but it's just like her to put herself in charge of everything."

"She always has been in charge of everything," I said. "Let's go worship at her feet – I'm sure begging will be involved – and go home."

"I'm with you," Thistle said. "Let's kiss her royal butt and get out of here."

"Has everyone forgotten who is in control here?" Mom asked, struggling to pull herself out of the narrow confines of her golden throne. Her dress was so wide it put up a fight. "I'm in control! I am! I have lists! Did you not hear me when I said I have lists?"

I shot her a sympathetic look. "I'm sure it's hard being you," I said. "I think it's hard being all of us, though."

"Even Aunt Tillie," Clove added.

I grabbed Landon's hand. "Come, my prince," I said. "We're done here."

We pushed past the guards, who conveniently pretended they didn't see us. We were halfway down the path that led to the castle when Mom launched into one of her patented diatribes.

"I'm so sick of this," she said. "I can't tell you how sick of this I am. I'm the queen! I'm in charge! Does anyone listen to me, though? Of course not. It's all about the great and powerful Tillie! She's the one everyone listens to. She's the one everyone fears. She's the one everyone bows to."

"Life sucks," Clove called over her shoulder.

"And then you die," Thistle added, laughing.

"I'm just sick of this," Mom said. "I have to wear this stupid dress and no one listens to me! Well ... I'm not taking one more second of this. I'm just ... done!"

I risked a glance back at Mom, a momentary surge of pity washing over me. "It will be better when we get home," I said. "As long as you haven't been eaten by zombies or anything, that is."

"Oh, I'm done playing nice," Mom said, throwing her crown on the ground and kicking it angrily. "I'm so done! Guards! Guards! Off with their heads!"

I froze at the command, and when the guards sprang into action I realized we weren't quite out of the woods yet.

"Run!"

DO you really think they'll kill us?" Thistle asked, leaning against the outside castle wall, gasping.

"I think we're safe as long as we can get inside the castle," I said, pushing her forward. "Move."

"I'm tired."

"The guards are still coming," Landon said, stepping beside me and grabbing my wrist. "We have to get inside the castle."

"Shouldn't there be more doors?" Clove whined.

"That would be too easy," I said. "Now, come on. We're so close I can almost taste it ... and by taste it I mean I can actually taste the real food waiting for us if we can manage to get out of this hateful place."

"I want bacon," Landon said.

"I'm going to glue bacon to my body and roll on top of you for an hour if we ever get out of here," I said.

"Sold," Landon said, increasing his pace. "The door should be around this corner. Come on."

"Are we sure that the castle is the way out?" Sam asked, pressing his hand against the small of Clove's back to prod her. Because she was the shortest she was having the most trouble keeping up. "What if we have to go back down the beanstalk?"

"The bears told me this castle belongs to Aunt Tillie," I said. "I believe them. They also knew about the sacrifice."

"Thanks for warning us," Thistle grumbled.

"Hey, you guys were already gone when we found out," I said. "Don't blame me for this. You could have screamed or something when they took you."

"They had their hands over our mouths," Clove said.

"And knives at our throats," Marcus added.

"Everyone shut up and run," Landon said. "There's the door."

"What do we do when we get inside?"

"We find Aunt Tillie and sit on her until she sends us home," I said. "I'm out of patience."

"And I want bacon," Landon said, hopping up the steps and throwing his body weight against the castle door to open it. "This is it. This is going to be the end. If it's not, I'm sitting down on the floor and never moving again. This is all I can take. This is … good grief. Will you look at this place?"

If your inner voice tells you something is too good to be true, tell it to shut up. Inner voices don't know anything but how to rain on your parade. They're real downers most of the time.

– *Aunt Tillie's Wonderful World of Stories to Make Little Girls Shut Up*

CHAPTER 19

"Whoever said you can never have too much green was lying," said Thistle as she screwed up her face while glancing around the castle foyer. "This is ... just ... horrible."

The castle had undergone yet another transformation. This one looked as though someone had put the Hulk in a blender and forgotten to put the top on before hitting the "puree" button.

"Look," Clove said, pointing at the floor. "The yellow brick road is back."

"I knew we were going to end at Oz," I said.

"You're very smart, sweetie," Landon said.

"And you always have to be right," Thistle added.

"Shut up, Thistle," I said.

"You shut up."

"Both of you shut up," Landon said. "This is crunch time, people. We need a touchdown. We all have to work from the same playbook."

"Have I ever told you how turned on I get when you use sports metaphors to rev us up?" I asked.

"No."

"There's a reason," I said.

Landon rolled his eyes.

"I think the bloom is off the rose for all of us," Marcus said. "We're struggling here. Landon is right, though. We're close. We only have to get through one more story. Can we please try to refrain from killing each other until we're all back in the guesthouse?"

"I can't make that promise," Thistle said. "I've been through a lot today."

"We've all been through a lot," Clove said.

"Not really," Thistle replied. "You got shoved in a tower for a bit and then got insulted by some dwarves who didn't like the way you sang. I had to kiss a frog."

"Thanks again, honey," Marcus said.

Thistle ignored him. "I also had to kill a wolf," she said. "I ate poisoned food and passed out. How does your day compare to mine?"

"You don't want to start comparing experiences," I warned.

"You definitely don't," Landon agreed. "You've all had it easy compared to us."

"Wah, wah, wah." Thistle danced around a little, something that was out of the ordinary – even when we weren't trapped in a book.

"We're being affected again," I said. "I'm not sure by what, but this is the last obstacle. We can't succumb to it."

Landon cracked his neck. "How can you tell?"

"Thistle just danced while insulting you," I said. "She's not big on dancing."

"She's right," Thistle said, glancing down at her feet. "I have horrible rhythm. I don't dance unless it's a slow one and I can let Marcus lead."

"It's the only time I get to lead," Marcus said.

"Join the club," Landon said, rubbing my back. "Okay, everyone, bite your tongues. Let's not talk unless we absolutely have to."

Everyone nodded and snapped their mouths shut. After a few minutes of staring at each other and hopping from foot to foot, I couldn't take it any longer. "That's not going to work."

"I'm sorry," Landon said. "That was a bad idea."

"Let's find the great and powerful Tillie and get out of here," Thistle said. "If I jump on her, someone pull me off before I kill her.

I'm afraid we'll be trapped here forever if I kill our 'Get Out of Oz' talisman."

"I'll let you get in a few good licks first," Landon said. "What? She has it coming."

"Did someone say my name?" Aunt Tillie materialized out of nowhere, popping into existence a few feet from us. She was no longer dressed as a fairy godmother, instead wearing a camouflage dress with a wide belt cinched at her waist. Her face was serene as she bowed in front of us. "Welcome to my home."

"I'm going to kill you, old lady," Thistle said, launching herself at Aunt Tillie and falling flat on the ground when Aunt Tillie disappeared.

"Where did she go?" Clove asked.

"I have no idea."

"Don't do that again," Landon ordered, wagging a finger in Thistle's face. "She obviously doesn't like being attacked."

"No, she doesn't," Aunt Tillie said, blinking back into existence on a velvet settee in the middle of the room. She glanced at her fingernails, feigning boredom. "Besides that, you can't catch me. I'm quick … like a ninja."

"I can if I make a really big rat trap and bait it with essence of evil," Thistle growled.

Aunt Tillie was nonplussed. "I don't think that's going to work."

"I do."

"I don't."

"I do."

"Let's get back on target, shall we?" Landon said, focusing on Aunt Tillie. "We're ready to go home."

"And where is your home?"

"Aren't you the great and powerful Tillie?" I asked. "Shouldn't you know that?"

"Who says I don't?"

"Why would you ask if you didn't know?"

"Why do you care?" Aunt Tillie asked. She was so annoying. Even her alter egos were obnoxious.

"We want to go home," I said. "We're really tired. We've worked our way through all the stories. I think we've earned our ruby slippers ... or whatever weird thing you're going to give us to get us home. I'm guessing with you we're going to be tapping combat boots together."

"What makes you think I can get you home?" Aunt Tillie asked. "I'm very good at what I do, but I'm not omnipotent."

"That's not what you usually say," Clove grumbled.

"Did you say something, dear?"

"I said your dress is beautiful," Clove said.

"That's what I thought you said."

"We've learned our lessons," I said, choosing my words carefully. "Now we want to go home."

"I'm not sure you have learned your lessons yet," Aunt Tillie said. "You might have one left to learn."

"No," Landon said, emphatically shaking his head. "No more lessons. We're good."

"Come on," Aunt Tillie purred. "The last one will be easy. I promise."

"What is it?" I asked, resigned.

Aunt Tillie pointed to a door at the far end of the room, and as if on cue a group of people moved through it. I recognized each and every one of them – and I actually wished I had a camera.

Marnie was there, struggling to move through her tin outfit as the joints made rusty creaking noises with every step. Chief Terry, dressed as a lion, held her steady at one side while a scarecrow that looked suspiciously like Twila gripped her other arm. A green-skinned witch (my mother is going to be furious when I tell her how she looked in this one) cackled like a mad woman while several flying monkeys – which bore a striking resemblance to Aunt Willa, Rosemary and Lila – flanked her.

"What are we supposed to do with them?" I asked, rubbing my forehead.

"Can someone tell me why I'm even here?" Chief Terry asked. "I wasn't part of any of this. This is embarrassing."

Landon shot him a sympathetic look. "I think she just had a leftover role to fill."

"At least you can walk," Marnie said. "Why am I the one who doesn't have a heart? I'm a very loving person."

"At least you have a brain," Twila said, miserable. "Why does everyone think I'm stupid?"

"Hey! I'm the one with green paint seeping into my pores," Mom snapped. "Do you have any idea how hard this crap is going to be to get off? Not to mention this is the second ridiculous outfit I've been dressed in – and both characters have been less than flattering."

"That's a nice way of saying you're a villain," Thistle said. "Don't feel bad. Everyone's been hinting that I'm a villain for the past … what … twelve hours? I'm beyond it."

"Clearly," I said. "It's not as though you're dwelling on it at all."

"Shut up, Bay," Thistle said.

"Can someone explain why I'm a monkey?" Lila asked.

"I think it's an improvement," I said.

"I'm never going to forget this," Aunt Willa said. "I have a long memory, and I'm going to make whoever did this pay."

"Shh," Aunt Tillie said, lifting her finger to her lips. "No one cares what you have to say."

Aunt Willa scowled. "This is so disrespectful."

"I kind of like it," Rosemary said, running her fingers over the fur. "It's warm and cozy."

"Shut up, Rosemary," Aunt Willa said. "No one asked you."

"I honestly don't get it," I said, shifting my attention back to Aunt Tillie. "What are we supposed to do with them?"

"You can kill me if you want," Chief Terry said, raising his hand and causing Marnie to pitch forward.

"Get me out of this outfit right now!" Marnie struggled to avoid toppling over.

"I have an idea," Thistle said, striding over to a table on the far side of the room. She yanked the green carnations from a vase and tossed them on the floor before walking over to my mother. "I'm really sorry about this." She tossed the water in Mom's face and took a step back.

"What the hell?" I couldn't believe she did that.

When Mom didn't immediately start melting I relaxed, if only marginally. "I don't think that worked."

"I'm going to ground you all within an inch of your lives," Mom said. "I'm going to put a whole list of punishments together and I'm going to love doling out each and every one."

"Ignore her," Aunt Tillie said. "She's talking nonsense – like always."

"Well, it was worth a shot," Thistle said, shoving the vase onto another table and flopping onto the settee next to Aunt Tillie. "I'm out of ideas. I want to go home."

Aunt Tillie smiled. "I didn't say you had to solve a puzzle," she said. "I said you had to learn a lesson."

"What lesson?"

"I can't tell you what the lesson is," Aunt Tillie said. "You have to figure it out yourself. That's how Tillie's World works."

"You named the book world after yourself?" Thistle asked, incredulous. "That's so … ."

"Genius?" Aunt Tillie supplied.

"I was going to say narcissistic," Thistle replied.

Aunt Tillie glared at her. "I don't need this. I'm a very busy woman. I don't have to sit here and take your abuse. I'm not the one who wants out of here."

"Oh, please, Aunt Tillie," I said, hating how whiny I sounded. "We're sorry. We're really sorry. We're sorry we yelled at you. We're sorry we threatened you. Heck, we're sorry we ever laughed at you. We're sorry for every rotten thing we ever did to you."

"Go on," Aunt Tillie said, clearly enjoying herself.

"We just want to go home," Landon said. "I've never wanted any one thing more than I want to be able to roll over … in a bed … and realize that I'm not alone and we're not about to be attacked by something or threatened by something or even simply annoyed by something."

His words tugged at my heart – and pricked at my brain. "We're ready to go home," I said, grabbing Landon's hand. "After all, there's no place like home."

Aunt Tillie jumped to her feet. "See! Was that so hard?"

"That's it?" Thistle's eyebrows flew up her forehead. "That's all you wanted?"

"I'm easy to please," Aunt Tillie said.

Thistle looked as if she was about to argue but Marcus wisely clapped his hand over her mouth. "You're very easy to please," he said.

Aunt Tillie winked at him and then waved her hands dramatically. After a brief burst of light, the rejects from Oz who resembled our family disappeared – along with the horrid green interior of the castle – and we found ourselves standing in an almost empty parlor. The only things in the room were two pedestals. A pair of ruby slippers sat on one and a gold lamp rested on the other.

"Which way do you want to go?" Aunt Tillie asked.

"Which one is quickest?" Landon asked.

"The shoes."

"We'll take the shoes."

"The lamp is more fun, though," Aunt Tillie said. "It involves a magic carpet ride through the heavens before you land back home in your beds. I hear it's to die for."

"I don't really care," Landon said. "I ... really? A magic carpet ride?"

Aunt Tillie nodded.

Landon glanced at me. "One more adventure couldn't hurt, could it?"

I smirked. "I don't think we'll ever run out of adventures," I said, linking my fingers with his. "I'm in for the magic carpet ride, too. I can't think of a better way to get home."

I BOLTED TO A SITTING POSITION, my eyes searching the inky black for a hint of movement or familiarity.

I was in a bed, although the quiet didn't offer any hints about whether or not it was my own. I instinctively reached to the other side of the mattress, almost crying when I felt the empty spot. Something moved beside me on the other side, and I felt Landon's arm wrap around my waist. "I'm right here, Bay."

"I ... where are we?"

"Home." He sounded sleepy.

"Did you just ... ?"

"Go to sleep, sweetie," he said, pulling me tight against him. "We'll talk about it in the morning."

"But ... ." Did that happen? Was it real? Was it a dream?

"Come on, princess," Landon murmured, settling me next to him and burrowing his face against my neck. "We'll have a new adventure to grapple with in a few hours."

Despite my uncertainty I gave in and cuddled into him. Even if this was a dream it was the best one I'd had in ... well ... forever.

"There's no place like home," I muttered.

"You're still giving me bacon in the morning."

A dream is a wish that hasn't come true yet. And sometimes it's just a bunch of crap that happened throughout the day jumbled up in a ridiculous way. Am I telling you not to dream? No. I'm telling you to dream big if you're going to do it. And sometimes … and this is extremely rare … but sometimes they do actually come true.

– *Aunt Tillie's Wonderful World of Stories to Make Little Girls Shut Up*

CHAPTER 20

I woke with a moan the next morning, every muscle in my body aching. I rolled over, groaning loudly, and found the bed empty. I pressed my eyes shut, waiting for the momentary sense of panic to wash over me. Landon wasn't there, but for once I didn't have even a sliver of worry.

I climbed out of bed, grabbing my robe from the floor and wrapping it around me before walking into the living room. Thistle, Marcus, Clove and Sam sat on the couch, pale faces highlighting four weary countenances and slouching shoulders.

I shifted my attention to the kitchen, smiling when I saw Landon standing behind the counter nursing a mug of coffee. Even though he usually woke up looking effortlessly handsome, there was some wear and tear on his features this morning.

His face brightened when he saw me. "Good morning, Sleeping Beauty."

"Nice," I said, shuffling toward the kitchen. Landon pressed a fresh mug of coffee into my hands before I even asked for it and dropped a soft kiss on my forehead.

"I'm sorry I left you in there," he said. "I didn't want to wake you, though, and I really needed some caffeine."

"It's fine," I said. "For once it didn't bother me."

Landon lifted an eyebrow, contemplative. "Maybe fairy tale world was good for a few things after all."

"Yup," I said, resting my head against his shoulder. "I learned I'm awesome under pressure."

As far as grins go, Landon's was beyond charming. "You are. How do you feel this morning?"

"I hurt," I said. "I wasn't sure whether … you know … everything was real until I tried to move. I think climbing that beanstalk took more out of us than we realized."

"Oh, I realized while it was happening," Thistle said. "Why do you think I didn't want to climb it?"

"I thought it was general laziness," I replied, wrinkling my nose.

Thistle stuck her tongue out and blew a raspberry in my direction. "Bite me."

"Maybe when I have more energy," I said.

After a few moments of silence, the only sound coming from occasional sips of coffee, I lifted my head and focused on Landon. "I can't believe you didn't go to the inn to stop Aunt Tillie from selling her wine."

"That seems like a futile endeavor after our adventure, doesn't it?"

I narrowed my eyes, a reaction he apparently found cute if his smile was to be believed. "I know you," I said. "Even though Aunt Tillie tortured and cursed us, you still wouldn't shirk your duties. Why didn't you run up to the inn to stop her?"

Landon cleared his throat before taking another sip of coffee. When I didn't move my eyes from him he gave in. "I had every intention of doing it," he said. "Until I picked up my cell phone and looked at the screen."

"I don't get it."

"What day do you think it is, sweetie?"

"Saturday."

Landon shook his head. "It's Sunday."

The gravity of his words washed over me. "No way."

"Yes, way," Thistle said, nodding her head. "We lost an entire day."

"We lost more than a day," Landon said. We lost a day plus eight hours. It really was the never-ending night."

"Well, technically it was day at the top of the beanstalk," I said.

Landon tilted his head to the side, confused. "I never really thought about that. It was definitely lighter up there, but there still wasn't any sun. It was like being stuck in a movie studio."

"Wow." I rubbed the spot between my eyebrows. "Are you ticked?"

"I'm so tired I don't even care," Landon said. "I hope she made a killing with her stupid wine." His stomach picked that moment to growl.

"Are you hungry?"

"Is that a trick question?"

"We should hop in the shower," I said. "Warm water might help our muscles, and we need to get up to the inn."

"What are we going to do up there?"

"Well, we need to check on our mothers," I said. "Also, I believe there's a bacon promise to fulfill."

Landon brightened considerably. "That's right. You're going to put it all over your body and roll on top of me."

"We'll do that next weekend," I said. "I ... I also need to talk to Aunt Tillie."

His body stiffened, but Landon's face was unreadable. "Okay."

"Aren't you going to ask why?"

"Nope," he said, draining the rest of his coffee. "I've learned you always have a reason for the things you do."

"How long do you think this great understanding of one another is going to last?"

"Until the next time we tick each other off," Landon said. "I think we have two weeks of bliss in front of us."

"Two weeks?"

"Give or take."

I couldn't stifle my giggle. "You make me laugh."

"I try. Now get moving. I feel dirty and I'm starving. Besides, you promised me a full day without any of your family. We can't honor all

219

of that, but we're going to do our best and disappear for the rest of the day after breakfast."

"I was actually thinking we could just disappear to my bed," I suggested.

"We're disappearing to bed," Landon said, "but we're going to another inn to rent one."

"Oh, I forgot about that. Do you still want to do that?"

"That's what's fueling me this morning," Landon said. "Move. Pack your clothes for the night before we go up to the inn. We're not coming back here. Not today at least."

"IT LOOKS QUIET," Thistle said, pressing her ear against the door to The Overlook. "What if they're still trapped somewhere?"

"Then they're going to be really ticked off," Landon said, reaching around Thistle and turning the door handle. "Come on. I'm starving."

"If they're not in here, you're not getting breakfast," Thistle reminded him.

"Oh, I'm getting breakfast," Landon said, wrapping his arm around my waist and lifting me off the ground so he could control our pace. "I've earned it."

After slinking through the back of the house – the family living quarters was cut off from the rest of the inn except for swinging doors at either end of the kitchen – we paused again outside of the kitchen.

The quiet was worrisome. And then … there was a noise. It was slight, but there it was. Someone moved a pot off the stove. I pushed the door open and stuck my head inside, exhaling heavily when I saw my mother.

Instinct took over when I caught sight of her and I hurried over and gave her a brief hug.

"What was that for?" Mom asked, surprised.

"I was afraid something happened to you," I admitted. "I … we … that is to say … ."

"We already know," Mom said. "You were cursed into the fairy tale book Aunt Tillie wrote when she was forced to read to you guys when you were kids."

"You knew and you didn't force her to let us out?" Relief at my mother's safety was turning to anger pretty quickly.

"We didn't know until this morning," Twila said, pushing Thistle's hair back on her forehead and studying her for a moment. "You look tired."

"I killed a wolf and rode a turtle."

"We fought zombies," Twila said. "Don't even start complaining."

"I knew it!" Clove said, pumping her fist. "I told you they were cursed into the zombie book."

"This whole family has a weird thing about being right," Landon said, moving away from me and heading toward the stove. He didn't even ask before grabbing three slices of bacon. Even though Marnie gave him a dirty look, he didn't back down. "I got turned into a monster and had to fight a giant. I'm hungry."

"Fine," Marnie grumbled.

"When did you get out of your book?" I asked.

"Overnight," Mom said, her tone clipped. "We checked on you guys immediately, but you were all asleep. That's when we found out everything that happened."

"Is Aunt Tillie still alive?" Thistle asked.

"She is."

"Does she still live here?"

Mom sighed, exasperated. "Of course she still lives here," she said. "She's family. You don't turn your back on family."

"Even when she puts you in mortal danger in a zombie book?" Clove pressed.

"Even then," Mom said. "I'm glad you're all okay, although you look exhausted."

"It's been a long thirty-six hours," Landon said. "And, just so you know, as soon as we're done with breakfast I'm taking Bay to a hotel for twenty-four hours – and I don't want to hear one complaint about it."

"Have fun," Mom said.

I'd been excited to tell her about her appearance in the fairy tales when I first saw her, envisioning a loud screaming match with Aunt Tillie. She looked beaten down, though. Now definitely wasn't the time.

"I'll be back tomorrow," I said.

"Take as much time as you want," Mom said. "I think we all need some ... space."

"Oh, you guys fought the entire time you were in the zombie book, didn't you?" Thistle asked. "I'm surprised you didn't kill each other."

"Let's just say it's been a struggle and leave it at that."

"Wow," Thistle said, laughing. "I thought we were grumpy until I saw you guys."

"You were in a fairy tale book," Marnie said. "You have no idea the horrors we saw."

"I think we have some idea," Landon said. "Our stories were ... unique."

Mom studied him a moment, a question on her lips, but she dismissed it. "I'm sure we can tell each other all about our adventures later. I don't want to talk about it now."

"I don't blame you," I said, patting her shoulder. "Everyone is still processing. I do have one question, though, and I'm almost afraid to ask it."

Mom waited.

"If you guys were in a book, and we were in a book, who ran the inn yesterday?"

Mom pursed her lips. "We got lucky that Belinda was here," Mom said, referring to a recent addition to The Overlook's staff. "She managed to hold things together all by herself. We really lucked out with her."

"We did," I agreed. "What did you tell her?"

"We told her there was a family emergency and we forgot to leave a note," Marnie replied. "I'm not sure she believes us."

"I wouldn't," I said. "Where is Aunt Tillie?"

Mom lifted an eyebrow. "Are you going to cause a scene?"

"Maybe."

"She's in the library."

"Aren't you going to warn me about making a scene?"

"Nope," Mom said. "Go nuts."

Landon and I exchanged a look. "Make sure you save me a heaping pile of bacon," he said. "I'm going with Bay. We'll be back in a few minutes."

We found Aunt Tillie sitting on the small couch in the library, a large leather-bound book resting on her lap. "Is that what I think it is?"

Aunt Tillie smiled at the sound of my voice. "How was your weekend? I haven't seen you guys since Friday night."

"How was your weekend?" I countered.

"Very lucrative," Aunt Tillie said. "I sold out at the Renaissance fair and made a killing. I didn't have one problem with law enforcement. It was a great weekend."

"For you," Landon said.

"You sound angry," Aunt Tillie said, smiling. "Is something wrong?"

Landon wasn't about to play her game. "I can see you wanting to punish me," he said. "Why did you purposely hurt Bay, Clove, Thistle, Marcus and Sam, though?"

"I didn't hurt anyone," Aunt Tillie said. "I gave you all a chance to expand your minds."

"By being beheaded?"

"You were never in any real danger," Aunt Tillie said. "You don't die in the real world if you die in the book. In fact, had you died in the book you would've simply slipped back into your regular lives. So, in theory, you should've all just offed yourself at the outset and saved yourself the aggravation."

Landon growled. "You're not even sorry, are you?"

Aunt Tillie seemed surprised by the question. "Why should I be sorry?"

"I guess if you don't know there's no sense in explaining it to you," Landon said. "I don't have the energy and I just ... you don't want to learn the lesson you were trying to teach us for yourself." He kissed the side of my head. "I'm going to eat breakfast. Don't stay in here too long. I wasn't joking about taking off right after breakfast."

"Okay," I said. "Are you okay?"

Landon graced me with a weak smile. "We're fine, sweetie," he said. "We just need some sleep and solitude. In twenty-four hours this is going to be nothing but a distant memory."

"That's not what I asked."

"I'm fine," Landon said. "I really am. Hurry up."

I watched him go, slowly turning back to Aunt Tillie when I was sure he was out of earshot. I had no intention of making a scene, but I wasn't about to let Aunt Tillie off the hook. I'd figured something out in my sleep, and I wanted to confirm it.

"I know the truth," I said.

"You'll have to be more specific."

"The book," I said. "That was really you in there. That was you who showed up to be my fairy godmother, and it was you who finally got us out. You go into the book all the time, don't you?"

Aunt Tillie shifted the book in her lap to the couch and got to her feet. "They need a benevolent ruler to lead them."

"That's not why."

"Then why?" Aunt Tillie was amused.

"You made them self-aware," I said. "They exist in the book. When we're not there, they're going on about their lives like they're real people ... or creatures. You created the book for us and it somehow got away from you. Admit it."

"I created the world for you and your cousins," Aunt Tillie corrected. "And you used to love visiting there. I thought you would like a return trip."

I was stunned. "I ... we've been there before?"

"I took you there for short trips all the time when you were small," Aunt Tillie said. "Those weren't just stories. They were memories."

"I don't understand. Why don't we remember actually being there?"

"You grew up," Aunt Tillie said. "You stop believing when you grow up. Although something tells me you won't forget this most recent trip."

"Everyone fought," I said. "Everyone got upset. Everyone got ... hurt. I think Landon got hurt most of all."

"If that's the case, I'm really sorry," Aunt Tillie said. "I really am. I needed a distraction. I didn't know he'd take it so hard."

"You knew," I said, "but I don't think you realized how bad things would get."

"How were they bad?" Aunt Tillie asked. "You saved each other at every turn. You gave up the ghost about your insecurities where he's concerned and he came to the conclusion that you're more than capable of taking care of yourself. How is that bad?"

My mouth dropped open. "Are you serious? Is that the real lesson you were trying to teach us?"

"I don't pick the lessons, Bay," Aunt Tillie said. "The book does. Those were the lessons you two needed to learn."

"Landon was right. You don't feel bad about any of this."

"I feel bad you were so stressed," Aunt Tillie said. "I don't feel bad about the rest of it, though. I warned you."

"I guess you did," I said, shrugging. I turned to walk away.

"That's it? You're not going to yell?"

"I'm not going to yell," I said. "It's not going to do any good, so why bother?"

"I thought you weren't going to give up the fight?"

"I'm not," I said, widening my berth when I saw Thistle loitering in the hallway with a red blanket in her hand. It was incredibly childish and yet ... somehow I was fine with it.

"Oh, now, come on," Aunt Tillie said, scampering behind me. "You can't stay angry with me. It's impossible."

I turned and watched her walk into the hallway. The second she rounded the corner Thistle jumped on her and wrapped the blanket around her head. "Who's fast now?"

"You get off me right now, Thistle Winchester," Aunt Tillie ordered. "Ow! That hurts. I'm old. You're going to break my hip!"

"I'm going to break your nose," Thistle said. "I can't believe you did that to us. I'm so angry I could kill you!"

"Get off me!"

"Make me."

"Get off me right now!"

"Make me right now."

I blew out a weary sigh and left Aunt Tillie and Thistle to their fight, joining Landon at the breakfast table.

"Is everything okay?" His face was calm but his eyes were stormy.

"I'm looking forward to our day together," I said. "Let's eat fast."

His eyes softened, twinkling a bit. "Do you want me to carry you around like a princess all day?"

"I'm the hero," I reminded him. "I'm going to carry you around."

Landon barked out a laugh. "Eat quickly," he said. "From the sound of that fight, Aunt Tillie is going to have twitchy fingers. I don't want to be here when they get loose."

Truer words were never spoken.

"Do you want to get breakfast someplace else?"

Landon considered the offer. "I'll race you to the truck."

Printed in Great Britain
by Amazon